The Vanishing Pearl

Broken Water Series

Book 3

Wentworth-by-the-Sea

Jennifer W. Smith

Published by ❍ Apple House Publishing
ISBN: 978-0-9966954-7-3

Copyright © Jennifer W. Smith, 2017

Editing by Sue Ducharme of TextWorks

Printed in the USA

DEDICATION

Hannah and Bradley

Novels by Jennifer W. Smith

Contemporary Romance

Flying Backwards

Landing in Love Series

Defying Gravity

Holding Pattern

Ground Control

Turbulent Kisses

Flight Plan

Falling in Love at Christmas: Holiday Special I

Protecting my Love at Christmas: Holiday Special II

Rescuing Love at Christmas: Holiday Special III

Paranormal Romance

Broken Water Series

The Rare Pearl: Book 1

The Forsaken Pearl: Book 2

The Vanishing Pearl: Book 3

Wiccan Haus Series

Legends Mate

Join my Book Squad – Facebook Group

Do you love sweet and sensual romances, and learning about the author who writes them? Join me!

Jennifer W. Smith's Book Squad

By joining you'll get access to early release Book Squad content and specials, learn the inside scoop about my books, and get to weigh in on my work-in-progress. Join Now!

THE HUMAN REALM

New Castle, New Hampshire

Harmony Parker — heroine

Pearl — Harmony's great-great-grandmother

Margaret Parker — Harmony's grandmother

Stanley Parker — Margaret Parker's husband

Harry and his wife — Friends of the Parkers, boat owners

Brook Parker — Harmony's mother

Eric — Harmony's father

Samantha Finch — Harmony's best friend

Mike Coombs — Acquaintance of Harmony's

David — Samantha's boyfriend

Rudy — Samantha's boss

Mary Falk — Finn's human mother

THE AQUAPOPULEAN REALM

The Coastal Clan on the Sacred Island
{New Castle, New Hampshire seashore}

Kodiak Night — Clansman Diver

Calder — Clan Linker

Nami — Calder's daughter

Binda — Calder's granddaughter and Linker

Rio — Calder's grandson

Morie — Keeper of the Wellness-by-the-Sea

Lynn — Wellness-by-the-Sea attendant

Deniz — Linker

THE AQUAPOPULEAN REALM

The Forest Tribe on the Great Falls
{Niagara Falls}

Finn Falk — Current chieftain

Nakoma — Previous chieftain

Umiko — Tribesman

Taura — Tribesman

Catori — Tribeswoman

Gale — Tribal Linker

Amadahy — Chieftain's room attendant

Bo — Farmer's son

Ren — Flower vendor's daughter

THE EARTHLY REALMS

Suijin — Water God

Luna — Siren

1

1989
The Human Realm

The headlights of Mrs. Coombs's sedan reflected off the chain-link fence that encircled the old Wentworth hotel. Numerous residents of the island were involved with the preservation committee to save what was left of the turn-of-the-century Victorian hotel. Mrs. Coombs headed the committee.

Mike sat in the front passenger seat next to his mother. He and Kodiak had just returned home from a shipwreck expedition, and he had gushed over every detail involved. From the backseat, Kodiak listened to Mike's long-winded rendition about their extended trip while his mother hung on to every word. Mike talked for the entire hour they traveled from Logan airport, where his mother had picked up the two young men, to the New Castle, New Hampshire, exit, where his mother took over the conversation. She spoke over her shoulder so Kodiak could hear while keeping her eyes on the narrow street, Wentworth Road.

Mrs. Coombs updated them about the Wentworth Hotel. "We've managed to get her on the Endangered Historic Properties list. But now, once again, the new company that bought her doesn't think they can renovate her." She referred to the Wentworth-by-the-Sea Hotel as *her*, as if the building were an old friend.

Kodiak ducked his head, looking out the window as they passed by the weathered, white-washed clapboards. In the twilight the building looked darker than dark, maybe how the iceberg looked to the passengers on the Titanic. The three of them had a common passion for

1

relics like shipwrecks and old buildings. Learning about the past gave insight to one's future, Kodiak thought. He sat back and grinned, thinking about his wife. She also referred to the Wentworth in much the same manner as Mrs. Coombs. There was no doubt the hundred-year-old hotel had an extraordinary history. Residents on this island seemed completely outraged that their piece of history was one wrecking ball away from demolition. He wondered how his wife was taking the news. He hadn't talked to her in weeks. He kept crazy hours on the expedition and took each opportunity to learn all he could, which meant late nights talking with the experts. Every chance he'd had, he tried to call her, but she hadn't answered. Bad timing, he'd surmised. Being under the water was in his blood—he was an Aquapopulean Diver, after all—though no one knew. He wanted to be included on future dives, and so he shook a lot of hands.

"What a shame," Mike grunted before he turned to look over the seat. He said to Kodiak, "Well, hopefully your return will cheer Harmony up. I know she's worked on saving that place for years."

Mrs. Coombs glanced at Kodiak in the rearview mirror. "Kodiak, please tell Harmony about the Endangered Historic Properties list. She wasn't at the last meeting."

Kodiak leaned forward. "Harmony missed the meeting?" He couldn't interpret the strange feeling that suddenly came over him. It was unlike Harmony to miss one of her Friends of the Wentworth meetings.

"Nope. I haven't seen her for a few weeks. What has she been up to?" Mrs. Coombs's curiosity was clearly piqued.

"Um, I'm not sure." Kodiak slouched against the seat, his eyes anxiously pinned on the road the headlights illuminated. "I haven't talk to her in a while."

In just minutes he would be home—well, the place he now called home, the house Harmony's grandparents left her. He missed Harmony so much he practically shook with excitement to think of seeing her. He thought about hearing her voice, seeing her smile, and feeling her body beneath his. He sat up straighter on the fabric bench seat. He couldn't wait to tell his wife how amazing his trip had been. But first, he just needed to know she was okay.

Mrs. Coombs pulled her sedan in front of the Parker house. Harmony's car was in the driveway, but the house was dark. "Do you have a key?" she asked Kodiak, concern in her voice.

"Yes, I can get in. I'm sure Harmony just turned in early," Kodiak said, opening the door. "Thanks again for the ride home, Mrs. Coombs. Talk to you later, Mike." He pulled his duffle bag off the seat and swung the car door shut. When he reached the back porch, he heard Mrs. Coombs drive away. Kodiak retrieved the hidden key and let himself in. He tentatively called, "Hello! Anyone home?"

After he switched on the kitchen light, he glanced around the room for any sign of his wife. Alarmed, he spotted what he was looking for. An envelope with his name in neat, loopy handwriting lay on the kitchen table. He dropped his duffle bag to the floor and rushed to collect the envelope. With one rip, he tore it open and plucked the note from inside. The envelope dropped to the floor unnoticed while his clumsy fingers worked to unfold the paper. The letter read:

Kodiak,
If you are reading this, then you have returned home before me. I was called away unexpectedly. I have gone to visit my relatives.

Don't worry, I will be back soon. I miss you—
please wait for me.

I love you,
Harmony

Kodiak read it through three times. His mind raced—
she couldn't have gone back to the other realm—she
wouldn't have! His long strides carried him to the study.
His webbed fingers flipped the light switch on the wall
that turned on a lamp by the window. The dish of herbs
lay exposed on the desk, confirming his fears. Harmony
had burned the herbs that miraculously sent her into the
other realm.

Kodiak's mind churned. Something didn't add up.

He glanced at the window but couldn't see anything
through the dark glass. The portal was out there, beyond
the lawn and the bay, under the Atlantic. He knew all too
well his beautiful wife was terrified of deep water; she
had told him she never wanted to endure that experience
again. Since her only living relatives resided in the other
realm, that clue confirmed her whereabouts. *Called
away? What could have lured her to go back?*

Several scenarios crossed his mind. Perhaps
Harmony's great-great-grandfather, Calder, had come
through the portal to tell her that someone was ill or
hurt? Maybe Calder was at his life's end; after all, he
was one hundred and twenty-six. Or...what if the clans
and tribes couldn't work out a peace treaty? Would
Calder or Finn expect Harmony to return and help them?
She alone was able to fight off the water god and his
sirens and sea serpents. Had the water god made himself
visible, demanding worship from the Aquapopulean
race? Had the sirens attacked, forcing the people to seek
Harmony's help?

Exhausted from traveling, Kodiak retrieved his bag and then mounted the stairs to their bedroom. With nothing to do but wait for her return, he crawled into bed. Sleep eluded him. He lay there, running his hand over the sheets on Harmony's side of the bed. He felt something like agony without her. Clutching her pillow to his face, he inhaled her lingering scent. A memory flooded his thoughts…

Kodiak's eyes followed Harmony as she moved around the room. She had not been his wife for long. The lavender pearl ring she wore, had always worn, was now her wedding ring. Kodiak reminisced that he'd gotten more than he'd bargained for the day she'd solicited his help on the beach. He risked his life on that journey to gather the herbs in sea serpent–infested waters and in the dangerous swamp and fields guarded by gigantic bears. But he had earned the ultimate prize, his stunning wife Harmony.

True, he hadn't wanted to leave his realm to take the perilous journey into the human world, but he'd had no choice. Harmony was going back, and he couldn't be without her. No woman had ever made him feel the way she did. He'd had his fair share of girlfriends, but Harmony was the most beautifully exotic and sweetly loving woman he had ever known.

She had just finished showering and wore her fluffy pink robe. Kodiak frowned, unable to visualize any part of her alluring shape. Her voluminous blond hair was still dry, piled haphazardly on her head. There were no blonds in his realm. Evolution there had produced only brunettes. He was about to beckon her, but she released her hair and picked up her hairbrush, stalling his words. He loved watching her brush her long hair. Mesmerized, he pictured running his fingers through it. She caught him staring at her in the mirror, and the corners of her pouty mouth turned up. That sweet mouth drove him mad—the cavern tasted sweet, and her playful tongue was always his undoing.

The superior gleam in her eye caused him to lie back, allowing his anticipation to build. Harmony's innocent and demure exterior hid her vixen qualities—that alone made his mind race with sinful thoughts. When she turned toward him his heart squeezed with emotion.

"Take that thing off and come over here." His voice was husky. His chest rose and fell with growing intensity.

Laugher rumbled in her throat as she placed her hands on the end of the mattress at his feet. Lifting one knee onto the bed, she moved forward slightly and placed her other knee on the bed. She poised on all fours, straddling his long legs. His foot lifted, and his big toe managed to loosen the tie of her belt. The robe was dangerously close to opening all the way. At her outraged huff, he smiled gleefully. She advanced like a prowling cat before she stopped, her head above his chest and her knees still straddling his legs. He lifted his hand, wanting to touch her soft hair, but she eased back on her heels, dropping her head to his belly. His hand paused in midair, his heart thudding, waiting for what she was going to do next.

Her eyes held his, innocent and sweet. She parted her lips and dropped a wet kiss on his muscled stomach. His body lifted slightly, as if doing a crunch, allowing her to kiss each ripple of muscle. Her hair tickled his bare chest and thighs. More kisses scorched above the band of his boxers. Her kisses moved torturously up his torso. When he felt her heavy breasts against him, skin to skin, he groaned. He plunged his hands into her hair to hold her still for a moment, but she wiggled. The friction caused him to suck in a breath.

Pressing up on her arms, she was above him on all fours. Her robe hung open, and all was his for the taking.

Her hair, like a lion's mane, hung against his chest. His fingers slipped through it. She shuffled enough to lean down and kiss his mouth. The kiss was soft and slightly hesitant, making him suffer with anticipation. It made his blood boil faster, and his hands reached to touch where her robe was parted. She sat back, pressing onto his lap. He watched her wicked grin, knowing and feeling what she was doing to him. *The minx!* He slid his hands inside the robe, filling his palms. The robe slipped from her shoulders, and she slithered her arms free. While his eyes feasted on her, his hand moved over her ribcage, feeling every bone. They traced the flare of her hips and the slender curve of her belly. His finger outlined her belly button and then slowly rose up through the valley of her breasts until his hand held the column of her regal neck. She arched back slightly caressing his thighs.

He pulled her onto him, recapturing her mouth. As he clung to her with fervor, he moaned her name between broken kisses. Maybe she'd sensed his urgency and longing—something made her lift her head. Her lips were parted and swollen from his assault, and her eyes questioned him.

Meeting and marrying someone within scarcely a week's time was uncommon, yet the attraction they'd felt for one another from the start was undeniable. He'd known for a while that he was in love with her. Coming here and getting to know her better confirmed it. He slid his hand into her golden locks again, caressing her silky back.

"Harmony…"

She became still, waiting for him to continue. He beheld her clean and glowing skin. He whispered, "You are so exquisite." She lowered her dark lashes, veiling her eyes.

"Hey," he coaxed, and her eyes met his once again. "I want you to know that crossing a realm for you is nothing compared to the way I feel about you. I love you, Harmony."

A wide smile filled her face before her mouth rushed his and his body flared to life once more. After all the turmoil of crossing the realms, he knew one thing for certain—he was completely in love with this mixed-race beauty from the human world.

But now she was in the Aquapopulean realm, lost to his longing touch.

2

1989
The Aquapopulean Realm

The tribal guide remained watchful and silent, making Harmony's trip long and unbearably quiet. Her guide would return home to the Forest city after he safely delivered her to the Wellness-by-the-Sea temple. Finally she'd return home. Once she crossed over into the human realm this time, she wasn't likely return to this realm again.

After Finn and Samantha's wedding and heartfelt good-byes, this week-long journey to the seacoast from the Great Falls provided Harmony with time to brood over various scenarios for how her delicate relationship with her husband could proceed. She had been gone from the human realm too long. Kodiak was expected to return home from the Lake Superior wreck expedition any time now. She longed to see her husband again. They were newlyweds, married five months. Adjusting not only to each other, to Kodiak, the human realm seemed less desirable than his own Aquapopulean realm. She found it encouraging that the diving expeditions interested him.

She envied Finn and Samantha, wishing her own relationship with Kodiak was so strongly connected. Not understanding how the cosmos worked, Harmony was further awed that her human best friend, Samantha, and her fellow kindred spirit Finn had been brought together.

Samantha had found her soulmate in Finn, the chieftain. Last summer after Samantha's horrible breakup and the loss of her job, Harmony had seen her friend suffering from rejection and the sting of unfairness. However, here in the Aquapopulean realm, Samantha had been renewed and happy—the kind of in-love happiness that made her glow.

Harmony wished she and Kodiak could have remained in this realm; she feared she'd lose him in the human realm. She understood that he felt lost, like a fish out of water. She'd felt the same way when she first came to the Aquapopulean realm. There were other compelling reasons to stay. Her only living relatives resided in this realm: her great-great grandfather Calder, Aunt Nami, and cousin Rio. Leaving Samantha, Finn, and their expected child was a hard choice, but she had to go back. Kodiak had sacrificed everything for her. She missed him so much that her chest constricted with grief at the thought of being away from him so long.

Harmony now floated in a canoe down the river toward the open sea. She rolled her neck, her body stiff with apprehension and from days of riding in the saddle on the back of an elk. This last portion of her journey was more bearable. They were nearing the sacred island. Only when the river widened did her fear of deep water resurface.

Inhaling deeply, she sighed. *Ahh, the smell of the ocean. We are back.* She closed her eyes, feeling the sun on her face, trying to enjoy the simple pleasures of nature. Crossing the realms was a precarious business, and she drew on positive energy to diminish her woes.

Suddenly her eyes flew open when canoe jerked sharply and she heard the unexpected sound of a loud splash. Her guide had vanished, paddle and all. She called his name and searched the river surface for any sign of him.

Nothing.

What is happening? Did he jump?

The canoe continued swiftly down the river toward the open sea. Swiveling her head to look all around, Harmony couldn't understand why she was traveling at such a high rate of speed. She'd never seen a current so swift as the canoe entered the mouth of the bay. Her heart pounded as she frantically computed her options.

Jump out and swim to the bank—no, the water is too deep! Call for help when I pass another vessel? Yes, there are many boasts in the harbor.

But her canoe whizzed past the other boats and continued to pick up speed. The thrust sent her sprawling on her back, glued to the floor by g-forces. She struggled to pull herself up, her white-knuckled fingers gripping the wooden seat. Her hair was flattened against her head by the wind, and her eyes watered. Everything was a blur.

What the hell is happening?

After ten minutes the canoe slowed to bob on the waves. Harmony grasped the sides and pulled herself up onto the seat. Shielding her eyes, she scanned the horizon line. She stifled a cry. She couldn't see land anywhere! Hands trembling and knees shaking, she blew out long, steady breathes. Her fear heightened when something moved in the water. Her panicky thoughts conjured real and threatening sirens or a sea serpent or...

Suijin lifted from the water like a statue rising from a fountain. It was *him*—the water god! He stood on the surface as though he were standing in a shallow puddle. Water droplets shimmered and danced on his taut skin. His black hair, smooth against the thick column of his neck, was slicked back from his handsome face. Physically he looked the part of a god, with the body of a gladiator, his face chiseled and well balanced. His bearing was confident and powerful. Harmony's terror dropped a notch. There was something about him that was...compelling.

During their last encounter weeks ago, he had warned her that he wanted her alone to spend time together. Lives had been at stake. She was pressed to agree. She depended on him to help her and her friends escape the swamp. Suijin kept his end of the bargain and brought them the boat they desperately needed, but then he'd disappeared. Apparently Harmony wasn't going to return to her realm without fulfilling her end of the agreement.

Suddenly she realized that Suijin had removed her guide and powered her canoe from beneath the vessel, taking her farther away from everyone she knew. He finally had her, helpless on the deep ocean she feared.

"I don't like being out here over deep water." Her voice quivered. "What do you want?"

"Harmony, I want us to get to know one another better," he said casually, as if they were chatting in a grocery store line.

"Can't we go back to shore? We can talk at the temple...or on the private beach," she suggested. "I promise to give you my full attention once we return to land."

Suijin seemed to consider her words. "Don't you like the water? You have Aquapopulean blood in your veins."

"No, I don't like *deep* water. And I'm only a quarter Aquapopulean. Please, can we turn back now?"

"We will not turn back."

"I need to return to the human realm. My friends are safe...and now I need to go home."

"You belong in this realm." In the bright sunlight his eyes appeared dark below his thick brows. They studied her intently.

She shook her head. "I have a husband in the human realm. He is waiting for me."

"Yes, the Aquapopulean Diver. He should not have crossed. He disobeyed the law." His dark brows rose in disdain.

Her eyes widened in surprise. "How do you know about him?"

"I know about everything that crosses through the realms," he stated matter-of-factly. "I will take you to my home where you will be more comfortable. We will have plenty of time to get to know one another better."

Harmony panicked. They were out in the middle of nowhere. *This god wants to take me to his home—what home? He might lock me away or kill me—like he did my family.*

Instinctively she reached into the satchel at her feet. She grasped the small tin that contained the herbs that would send her into the other realm. The portal lay just off the shore of New Castle, New Hampshire. She contemplated making a "run" for it. Maybe she could light the herbs and get back home before he could take her anywhere. Harmony knew the god could travel through the portal, but she didn't know how—perhaps he used the herbs too. Jamming her hand into her pocket, she curled her fingers around the Bic lighter she'd brought with her from the human realm.

"Fine. Is it close by?" Her voice was high.

"I will get us there as quickly as I can," he replied, and the corners of his mouth lifted.

She nodded, waiting for him to return under the water. As he slowly sank into the waves, she shifted in her seat and brought the tin to her lap, hiding it in the folds of her clothes. Hoping the sea air wouldn't hamper the effects of the smoke, Harmony gently popped the lid. As soon as he was out of sight, she planned to drop to the canoe floor and use her body to block the wind as she lit the herbs. She willed her hands to stop shaking.

The god sank to his waist, and he lifted his arm and swept it through the air. A swell came out of nowhere and rolled the canoe dangerously on its edge. With both hands, Harmony gripped the yoke; the tin toppled from her lap into the sea. The cover, which she had loosened, separated, and the contents sprinkled on the water, looking like fish food. Each leaf soaked up water before it sank. The tin's base and cover floated just out of reach until a white cap ate them.

As the canoe righted, she screamed, "No!" On her knees, she peered over the edge, but her vision couldn't penetrate the dark water. *They're gone! The herbs to send me home are gone!* She covered her face as her mind raced. It *was* possible to get more, but it had taken weeks to gather the ingredients before, and she'd had Kodiak, a Diver, Binda, and Rio to help her. *I don't have that kind of time!* Dropping her hands, she focused on the god, who watched her. He was calm and steady; his large hand rested on the canoe deck.

He asserted his control over her situation. "I'm not ready to let you go home."

Tears blurred her vision, and she only saw the outline of his form slip under the water. The canoe jerked forward to resume its accelerated skim across the ocean. She resolved to hunker down on the canoe floor to ride out the journey.

Harmony's lower lip trembled. She chided herself. *This is what I get for making a promise I did not plan to keep. Why does he want to spend time with me anyway? What's so special about me?*

Harmony encountered him four weeks ago. After she built up enough courage to go after her missing friend Samantha and cross the water portal, she had come face to face with Suijin once again. However, this time he'd come to her aid. Not only had he pulled her from the water and kept her from drowning, he'd brought her to

Cape Cod to save her friends. Later he'd protected her from the giant alligators and rescued her from Venus-fly-trap-like creatures. Finally, he'd provided a boat for her and her friends to return to the sacred island.

I should owe him, right?

Maybe.

Unfortunately, he did murder my mother and grandmother...and who knows who else. Is it possible to forgive something like that?

Over the years, every member of her meager family had drowned. When Harmony was a child, she and her mother had fallen through the ice, and she'd witnessed Suijin dragging her mother down into the inky blackness. She'd repressed the memory for years, until she'd crossed the realm and strange things began happening to her. Honestly, she didn't remember her mother, and she couldn't miss what she didn't remember. Her grandmother has raised her, and she still missed her terribly. But after her grandfather died her grandmother had changed. Margaret Parker had lost the light in her eyes.

The last of her generation in the human realm, Harmony was positively stunned to find she had relatives in the other realm. More astounding was the fact that she was the product of a race altered by evolution. Aquapopulean blood ran in her veins. And she wasn't the only one.

The canoe moved like a high-speed train, and Harmony's thoughts regressed into memories. In her mind's eye, the tall evergreens came into view and then the stone city on Niagara Falls, known as the Great Falls in this realm. Finn was chieftain of that land now.

A week ago Harmony and Samantha had said their teary good-byes, and Finn hugged her with conviction.

"Take care of her," Harmony said to Finn, who cast a loving glance at his wife.

"I will protect her with my life, and our children too." He had hinted at his aspiration for an extensive family.

Harmony had raised her eyes toward the sky, where the clouds floated, fluffy and bright. "I will think of you both every time I look at the clouds. I will look for the shapes of this place. Like that one," she pointed upward. "A lion."

"You know you could always bring Kodiak back," Finn suggested.

"I can't trust that everything regarding the Wentworth hotel is settled. I want to be sure the new company rebuilds it, as they say they will, so your realm doesn't suffer again. I will continue to fight on that front," Harmony reassured him. Then she said less enthusiastically, "As for Kodi...I don't really know what he wants. So much has changed for him...and I feel responsible. Even if he could survive the return trip, I'm not sure he wants to come back. Anyway, I need to go back to him and help him find balance."

"You take care of yourself, kitten." Finn's brotherly grin warmed Harmony. She would miss them both profoundly.

After a few days, Harmony and her guide had approached the tribal trading village at the edge of the Hudson River. As they crossed the bridge into clan territory, Harmony looked south to where she had once called upon the sirens to kill the entire group of tribesmen and women who had chased her, Kodiak, and Finn during her first encounter with this realm. The guide took her along the main route, stopping at various trading posts each evening, as she had done on her way to the city with Finn and Samantha. By the time they arrived at the last post and had traded the elk for a canoe, Harmony felt nothing but apprehension. She missed Kodiak but was terrified he would want to ditch her for his newfound freedom in the human realm. They hadn't been together that long, and during that time their relationship had been rocky. Although he swore she was his most precious treasure, maybe he hadn't understood how much treasure there was to choose from—both physical and material.

3

The canoe hit solid ground. Sitting up, she gasped with relief and then scrambled out of her floating prison onto the sand. She jogged up the beach until she reached the tall grass. She shielded her eyes and noticed an apple orchard not far from the tall waving grasses. When she glanced back over her shoulder, she noticed the canoe drifting out to sea. There was no sign of Suijin. She watched, but he didn't emerge from the water. She pressed into the interior, where apple trees grew abundantly. She wandered through the orchard, and on the other side she saw a path leading between evergreen trees. Cautiously investigating, she was pleasantly surprised when the path opened into a clearing around a simple waterfall and modest lagoon. Suddenly she licked her lips, realizing how thirsty she was. Fresh, cool water poured over the rocks, and she knelt to take a drink.

Her thirst quenched, she sat on her heels and listened for any sign of life. Confirming she was alone, Harmony wandered back through the orchard to pick an apple from a tree. What was she supposed to do now? *Where has Suijin gone?* He wanted her here, but he was nowhere to be found. Reaching the beach, she sat in the cool sand. The sun was setting, the sky awash with pink and orange bands.

"Why are you doing this!" she yelled to the waves. She didn't expect an answer, but Suijin appeared in the surf and strutted out of the water toward her. She noticed again his glistening broad shoulders and the chiseled chest that narrowed to his square waist. His hips were barely covered by the loin cloth she'd seen before. Breathless, she scrambled to her feet and squeezed the apple in the palm of her hand. Should she run back into the orchard? He looked determined to intercept her. Her chest heaved as she backed away.

"Stay away from me," she warned, and then she threw the apple at his head. He kept right on coming up the beach, merely tilting his head to avoid the flying object.

"This island is my home, and you are welcome here. I've just informed my companion that you are here. She is preparing your room. We can walk to the palace. It's just beyond the orchard in that direction." In the dwindling sunlight, his statuesque form cast long shadows.

His companion! Maybe there is someone there who can help me escape if he doesn't let me go.

He reached out to direct her. Aware she could use her abilities to keep him at bay, she lifted her hands and flexed her fingers, waiting for the heat to build, but nothing happened. She wiped her sweaty palms on her tunic and tried again. Nothing. No heat. No energy.

Where the hell is my power—my magic? Why can't I deflect him?

"It is okay. I'm not going to hurt you. You are my guest, Harmony." His expression softened, his grin meant to make her feel at ease.

She ignored him. "Why isn't this working? It worked before!" she cried in panic. She'd been able to burn him with her touch and physically send a pulse to force him away. She still had much to learn about her new abilities, but she was sure this one had worked! What was she doing wrong?

"I've taken a man-like form. Your abilities won't work on me when I'm transformed, so I'm not vulnerable to your scorching touch. I will take on this form while you get to know me and learn to trust me. Relinquishing some of my abilities to take this form should prove to you I'm genuinely trying to reach you.

See, no scales," He held up his arms, turning them about, and then showed her his hip and muscular leg, without scales for the first time. "Come, I'll take you to the palace," he said sincerely.

From god to man—he was a vision of human male perfection. But she didn't trust him. And she had no way of fighting him off without her mystical energy. It was starting to get dark, and she couldn't stay on the beach all night. *Yes, maybe someone at the palace will help me,* she hoped.

"Fine, but I can't stay long." She propelled herself in the direction he indicated, taking the lead. After five minutes through the rows of apple trees, she slowed her marching pace and walked easily beside him. She scrutinized him in her peripheral vision. At this moment, his nature seemed unthreatening and easy. He'd said that he wanted her get to know him and to trust him. Harmony wondered what taking human form had cost him. By eliminating her weapon, what had he given up? He hadn't changed much physically, besides losing his scales.

Would he tell her if she asked? Curiosity finally got the better of her. "What is the benefit of you taking human form? What's the tradeoff?"

He turned his head without breaking stride, and his extraordinarily beautiful smile took her breath away.

He answered, "Everything is a tradeoff. It is difficult for me to change physically, and it challenges me mentally when my powers are limited. But the tradeoff...well, the physical things I feel in return are... raw...exposed...pleasurable. Making love in man-like form, powerless, gives me unmeasurable gratification."

Mesmerized by his moving lips, she gulped in fresh air. What was happening to her? *I don't need that visual! Our playing fields are definitely not even.*

It appeared he held some power over her. His magnetism and attraction were potent, different from what she felt for Kodiak. Instinctively, her fingers slid around the lavender pearl wedding ring that had belonged to her grandmother.

Beyond the orchard, the land sloped before them and stretched across a wide field. Tramping through the overgrown grass, she remembered the turmoil she'd felt when she first met Kodiak. Though attracted to him, she'd vowed to dislike him because he had bargained for the very ring on her finger, but she fell in love with him regardless.

Kodiak—I need to get back to him. I must find out what this god wants with me so I can go home.

"Why did you take me? Is this what you do with everyone you've taken? With my family?"

"No, I don't bring anyone here. The family you speak of are gone, Harmony. Their souls were released into the universe to reunite with loved ones. They no longer suffer in the confines of their earthly bodies."

Harmony guessed there couldn't be a more pleasant way to think of her family leaving her life than to live on peacefully in the cosmos. Knowing her grandmother was with her grandfather again was a comforting thought, as was her mother and father's reunion. *But why am I different?*

"And me? You didn't kill me or release me from my earthy body. What do you plan on doing with me?"

"You, Harmony, are very special. I knew it that day when you and your mother fell through the ice. When you used your extraordinary power to keep me from you—it drove me mad. And what was more amazing was that you used your ability in the human realm!"

She rounded on him. "My mother and grandmother never hurt anyone. They were my family. You drowned my mother in front of me! You took her away from me—I was just a child! Did it matter that they were mixed-race?" Harmony's moods were swinging, as if she'd taken some tainted drug. The reality of two realms, a god, and abilities she didn't know how to control was messing with her psyche. The worst part was that she sometimes felt attracted to this murderer. She felt sick!

Eager to make her understand, Suijin explained. "Evolution always finds a way to alter life. Linkers mated with humans throughout the past, but not until your great-grandmother did a human become impregnated by an Aquapopulean Linker. As halflings, your mother, grandmother, and great-grandmother did not possess any abilities. Balance was compromised. They needed to be released. I consider myself a keeper of the portal gate. I should have ended the first woman's life when she became pregnant, but I waited, hoping no additional births would result—but they did. I am glad that my hesitation afforded me the chance to meet you, Harmony. I believe you've been sent to ease my eternal loneliness."

"Well, you are *wrong*. And what about my father's life? He was a *human* fisherman when his vessel sank. And my grandfather—his car plunged off the bridge, and he was trapped underwater. He was *human* too."

"When the opportunity presented itself, I released them as well. I watched you and waited for you to mature. Only then did I release your caregiver. The human realm is overcrowded, corrupt—inferior to the Aquapopulo race. I needed you alone, isolated in that realm, to show you that this is the realm for you to flourish in."

As she stumbled over a thick patch of grass, Suijin steadied her elbow. Jerking her arm away, Harmony remarked sarcastically, "And you are the judge of what realm is better... which race is worthy? You judge who should live or be released? What kind of god are you?

You don't sound like one I'd like to know." She turned away from him and continued marching, fury blinding her.

Arrogant god! Murdering my family! Bringing me to this forsaken place... It's too much. And for what exactly? To ease his eternal loneliness! What the hell does he expect me to do? Whatever!

Right now, she just wanted to put as much distance between them as possible. Harmony looked back over her shoulder at the orchard; it was far behind them now. Avoiding the brooding man-god beside her, she glanced ahead to see how much farther they needed to walk. The hill they'd been heading for was closer now, in clear view. A town curved up to its peak, and at the top a palace extended into the evening sky, its tower walls silhouetted against the setting sun. It reminded her of a place she'd studied in her architecture history class, Mont-Saint-Michel in France. The hill was dominated by a vast complex of buildings perched on protruding foundations. A platform of ivory-colored granite made up the base of the circular city. A wharf with massive docks rested at the base of the hill. From what she could see, sections were missing, and the docks needed heavy repairs. There were no boats—not one—which seemed sad to her.

When they approached the path from the field that led to the town, Harmony sensed something was wrong. It was too quiet. They passed through a modest archway into a courtyard. She scanned the empty buildings for people, animals, any sign of life.

The road they traveled rounded the mountain at a steep slant, and the views of the ocean between unoccupied shops became more beautiful as they ascended. Her anger subsided as her curiosity magnified. The shops were not just closed, they were vacant. Where had the people gone?

4

The Tribal City
The Aquapopulean Realm

In the days after Harmony left, Finn settled in with his human wife. Council meetings were going well, and the tribe supported his new leadership role. The hunters seemed to love their new female member. They enthusiastically showed their approval when Samantha exhibited her skills with her bow and arrow. Both women and men flocked to Samantha, who was a natural crowd pleaser. Finn read every man's face when Samantha walked by, her unique golden hair an eye catcher. The children swarmed her as she diligently learned each of their names.

Finn mused over the unlikely tangle of events that had brought his lively bride into his life. He didn't like to admit it, but his father, Gale the Linker, who had committed several crimes, had managed to bring Samantha through the portal and ultimately brought them together. Finn's father had mistakenly kidnapped Samantha, thinking he was bringing Harmony Parker back. Born marked as a Linker, Gale could travel between the realms.

With their long blond hair, Harmony and Samantha could pass as sisters. While Harmony had Aquapopulean blood, Samantha, merely human, had almost died after the crossing. The crazy thing was that when Gale revealed his true identity as Finn's father, Samantha forgave the man. Not only that, but she'd gone to Gale in the tower, persuaded the guard to let her into his room, and then told him to make amends with his son. When the guard had bolted down the corridor to tell Finn that

Gale had escaped, that Gale had gone to the human realm, Finn had been furious. But when he reached the tower and found the note his father left him, unnatural feelings rushed through him. His father felt proud of him—how could that thought touch Finn so deeply?

When he brought the note to Samantha, she confessed. "I spoke with Gale. I wanted him to do right by you. I wanted to tell our children something good about their grandfather."

It was crazy how much he adored this woman, even with her meddling and stubbornness. She had the talent to reach an evil man.

Finn appointed his longtime friend Umiko to not only continue to serve on his council but be his wife's personal bodyguard. Months ago his trust in his friend was tested, but in the end Umiko had proved loyal. He'd been led astray by Finn's father. Umiko thought his actions would further the tribe's prosperities, but Gale the Linker's ideas were too radical and would have disturbed the peace between the clans and the tribes. Umiko's other fault rested in his interest in Finn's wife. However, Finn understood Umiko's honor; the fact that he cared for Samantha would bind him to protect her with his life. And the warrior had pledged his life when he asked Finn to forgive him.

The two men stood in the map room discussing the road expansion to the salt mines. Umiko moved to the window when he heard the arriving hunters, a typical daily occurrence. But something seemed different—their speed. Finn heard it too but lingered over the map rolled out across the trestle table.

"Finn, you should see this," Umiko said in his usual deep monotone.

His concentration lost, Finn abandoned the scroll. Moving to the window, he saw a hunting party rapidly crossing the bridge, causing pedestrians to hurry out of the way. Within the group of trotting elk an odd man was among them. Finn focused on the man's tunic and knew immediately he was from the coast—a clansmen. He realized there must be trouble. Finn returned to the table and rolled the map. Umiko waited for him to return it to the wooden structure that held the maps. Umiko nodded at Finn, ready to follow him down to the receiving room.

When Finn entered the hall, usually filled with tables laden with fruit and refreshments for the city goers, a large crowd was already gathered. Instinctively, he scanned the room for his wife, but she wasn't there. A clan member, covered in dust, his shoulder-length hair falling in tangles, sure signs of riding hard, drank thirstily.

"Chief, this man has come to warn us that Harmony Parker's guide was found washed up on the riverbank, barely alive. Their Linker has healed him, and he is resting at the temple. However, he claimed as they were nearing the mouth of the river at the end of their journey, the water god pulled him from the canoe. Before he lost consciousness, he saw the water god take Harmony in the vessel out to sea," explained one of the hunters who'd just ridden in with the clansman.

Finn faced the clansman. "Are you certain? Did Calder send you?"

The man nodded. "Calder fears devastation might befall us all unless she returns to her realm."

"Umiko," Finn called above the din, "where is my wife?"

"In the weaving hall."

"Fetch her. Bring her to my rooms. I must prepare the warriors to leave for the coast within the hour."

Umiko strode away with purpose.

Finn called his trusted brothers at arms. After gathering the mounts, weapons, and provisions they'd need, Finn returned to his room. Samantha stopped chewing on her thumbnail when he rushed over to her.

"What's going on?"

"It's Harmony."

"What? Did she come back? Did she decide to stay in this realm?"

"She is still here, but not by her own choosing. Apparently the water god Suijin intercepted her canoe and carried her out to sea," he growled.

"No!" Samantha resumed biting her nail and appeared to concentrate. Looking up at him with dread, she confided, "She made a deal with him, Finn. Harmony told me when she spoke to the water god that he said something about her spending time with him. She agreed—if he'd help us." Samantha's brow was creased with worry. He reached for her, and she wrapped her arms around him. She mumbled into his shirt, "She did it to save us."

"I'm going after her. I don't trust that he won't kill her, like he did the rest of her family."

He felt his wife's head nod against his chest. "Be careful. You are going up against a god," she moaned, fear evident in her voice.

Finn slipped his hand through her golden hair to stroke her neck. His eyes swept over her lovely features before he pressed his lips to hers. The kiss, though it lingered, wasn't enough, but there was no time for more. He pulled away and opened the door. Umiko stepped into the room.

"Umiko, I'll need you to look after my wife while I'm gone."

"She will be safe, Finn," Umiko said without hesitation. "Beware, my brother, and safe travels."

Finn grabbed Umiko's forearm, and they exchanged nods. After one lingering glance at his wife, he slipped through the door.

After several weeks searching along the east coast, Finn returned home, leaving the clans to take over the effort. Harmony Parker was still missing.

5

Suijin's Island
The Atlantic Ocean

Suijin watched Harmony stray to the open doorway of an old shop. The glass was gone from the windows, and the wind whistled through the cracks. If he wanted to impress her, this abandoned town apparently wasn't the way to achieve that. He could have lifted her into his palace on a dazzling rogue wave, avoiding the desolate carcasses of these buildings.

He could have crumbled these buildings with pounding waves long ago, but he hadn't. He left them as a reminder of the nature of earthly man—not much different from the nature of the gods. Both were selfish.

By altering his divine state to a man-like form, he temporarily surrendered some of his powers. The now-invisible scales was the only physical sign; allowing his abilities to weaken was far more dangerous and extreme. Gods *never* gave up power. However, he'd considered it necessary. If Harmony couldn't use her ability against him and saw his humanity, perhaps she could connect with him. Her ability was truly miraculous, which made him wonder if she'd been gifted to him by another god, one who had possessed him in a way he wished to possess Harmony. He was willing to try this approach to appeal to her. At times he saw something other than hatred or distrust in her eyes when her gaze lingered on him. But he expected that he needed more than good looks and godly status. His palm cupped his elbow. His skin felt strange without scales. He followed her inside.

The nostalgia of being in the shops reminded Suijin of long ago, when he'd lived among the Aquapopuleans on their sacred island. They'd looked to him as their leader at first. He used his powers to drive in hordes of fish for the village to eat and taught the Linkers where to find healing plants. These gifts, which he gave freely to the people, brought him praise and gratitude in return. Soon praise morphed into offerings. They honored him by naming their children after the water he'd come from and sent their deceased into the water to complete their life circles. He'd explained to the Linkers that he'd come from the universe and was here now to watch over the realms.

It was natural to take his place as their god, but he found the alienation unsettling. He wanted to be included instead of worshipped from afar. The people eventually approached him to ask him to help with crop growth, fertility, and healing. He'd been happy to help before, but the dynamic of their relationship had started to vex him. Declining their request, he felt he had to separate from the people for a time. When he returned to the sea, they followed him in their vessels. When they encountered the island where Suijin went to think in isolation, they'd offered to build his kingdom there. In hopes that the people would change, he'd reluctantly agreed. And so the island city was born. He'd lived there contentedly with his people for a while. But nothing ever stays the same. He had wanted to fit in, be a member of their growing society. But it proved impossible. As he watched the race expand their villages, mate and reproduce, it distanced him further. He longed to have a partner.

"Where have all the people gone?" Her voice echoed in the empty chamber. The temperature was cooler out of the sunlight.

Suijin's smile was sentimental as he remembered the city in its heyday. "This city was once a thriving metropolis. The clans built the palace and surrounding community in my honor. I lived among the

Aquapopuleans for centuries. For thousands of years, they mined granite from the mainland and floated it here, toiling to build my kingdom."

His smile faded, and he murmured quietly, "Nothing lasts."

Harmony had been circling the room, examining the store's shabby remnants. She stopped at the shift in his voice and gave him her attention. He continued. "Many people moved back to the mainland after the sirens came. It was a strained relationship for both the Aquapopuleans and the sirens. Still is," he added, disappointment in his voice.

Harmony nodded, her lips pressed together. Suijin read her distasteful expression.

Suijin mindlessly stoked his arm as he continued to speak. "Before the last of the clans left, the council was formed. The council concluded it would be best if I stayed behind with the sirens. 'We built this for you. You should stay,' they insisted with devotion. Not long after they returned to the east the council became divided. Some left their sacred island and built another city on the nearby Cape. Suddenly they wanted to inhabit their own lands, where they were not under the thumb of their god." Suijin moved to the stone counter, recalling that the merchants who'd occupied this space once sold fishing spears and nets. He'd visited this shop on occasion during the city's prime.

"So... you were there when both races started, before this place, at the beginning of human and Aquapopulean evolution?" she asked, a hint of awe in her voice.

He tilted his head to gaze at the ceiling, remembering back through the ages. "I lived alongside both humans and Aquapopuleans at the water's edge. Both races discovered the seas could protect and feed them. Eventually humans moved onto the land for good. Naturally, I stayed more often with the Aquapopuleans.

Many generations later, when the Aquapopuleans transitioned to land, they worshipped that site as a sacred place. They built a temple, but it is not sacred to me." Shaking his head, he grimaced. "It's neither the temple nor the island that is sacred—it is the portal. The portal is the equilibrium of these miraculous worlds. And yes, they honor me in frivolous ways." Again he shook his head. "But they exclude me. They are feebleminded."

"So they shouldn't worship you? Fear you?" she questioned cautiously. Harmony kept her distance from him, moving away when he stepped closer. When she spoke of fear, she squared her shoulders, as if to silently declare she didn't fear him.

"I don't want their worship." he confirmed. "They fear they've persecuted me. Angered me." He raised dark eyebrows and admitted, "I am not pleased with them."

"You allowed them to leave?"

He shrugged and moved back to the doorway. "They shut me out, preferring to worship from afar. I still went to them, offering to ease their daily burdens." His frame easily filled the doorway. He ran his hand along the top of the doorjamb, feeling the stone crumble between his fingertips. "I *never* wanted their worship," he admitted.

Suijin narrowed his eyes at the last of the sunlight, eager to change the subject. "We'd best be getting to the palace. I promise it won't look like this." He stepped back from the doorframe so she could pass through.

By the time they reached the palace's grand door, it was dark. *This palace must have been impressive ages ago,* Harmony thought. Its stone façade was cracked; the foundation had sunk in places, leaving doorways oddly askew. Suijin swung open the door and retrieved a lit lantern, one of many on a large wooden trestle table opposite the door. Leading her down several corridors, he stopped when she stammered, "Sir…Suijin…Lord…"

The hallway was dim, so he lifted his lantern so she could see his face. He had no problem seeing in the dark.

She frowned. "What do I call you?"

He leaned forward, a foot between them, so she could see his expression. He lowered his voice as if telling a secret. "I hope one day you'll refer to me as 'my love,' but for now Jin will do." He got the reaction he'd expected. Her eyes widened before her lashes swept downward, and she refused to look at him. His deep voice and intimate words likely sent a shiver down her spine, he thought.

Pretending to be nonchalant, she ignored his talk of love and asked, "Jin, you mentioned sirens. Are they still here?" She made a show of hugging her arm and inspecting the darkness over her shoulder.

"Yes. They are my companions. Those feminine souls have not forsaken me." He saw his point wasn't lost on her. He still felt slighted that the clans had separated from his town and asked him to stay behind.

She followed him through the hallways as he spoke over his shoulder. Harmony tried not to lag behind his long strides to stay close enough to hear about the sirens.

"After the clansmen left the city it fell into disrepair. The sirens took up permanent residence along the cove and in the caves under the island, but they come and go as they please. One particular siren has been with me a long time. She has the special ability to walk on land, and so she lives here in my palace as my personal companion."

"How is that possible? I understood they can't leave the water."

"They can if I've given them the ability."

She was at his shoulder now. "You can give sirens the ability to *walk*?"

"Yes." His lips pulled to one side. He thought she was handling this new information quite well. She didn't seem frightened by the sirens, likely because of her ability to burn their skin and kill them. The sirens would be afraid of her. He felt the need to protect them.

"Harmony, you must refrain from using your abilities on them."

She shrugged a shoulder and nodded reluctantly. "As long as they stay away from me, which should be easy, since I won't be going in the water."

He accepted that answer for now. He closed the subject by asking, "Are you hungry?"

"Um...I haven't eaten since this morning."

"This way." He'd given her food for thought, but he wanted to make sure she ate real food and was well cared for under his roof. Entering a large kitchen, Suijin set the lantern on the table and opened a cupboard. "Help yourself to anything you want to eat."

She peeked in at the jars and boxes of food. Beneath the cabinet was a bucket piled high with apples. She chose one. She automatically rubbed it against the fabric of her tunic to make it shiny before she took a bite. He lifted one and mimicked her motions. He watched her glance at the shelves. Her gaze stopped at a jar of dried leaves.

"Would you care for some tea? I brought that back from the Orient in your realm not too long ago. I think it's still fresh. And we have honey collected from the hives by the apple orchard."

"No. I'm tired. I guess I'm not returning home tonight, so if there is a place I can rest, I'd appreciate it," she said honestly.

"Your room should be ready. I'll take you to it."

He led her up several staircases, listening to her weary breathing. No one person had captured his interest like Harmony had. No other human, Aquapopulean, or mystical being had set in motion the longing he felt for her. He had the power to make his mate immortal. He'd extended the lives of the sirens that he cared about over many centuries. He'd been with women of both races in both realms. They'd come to him in a worshipful way, eager to please him and fearful if they didn't. Harmony was the only being from a line of females conceived by a human and an Aquapopulean. She was different—she possessed unnatural powers in *both* realms. When she was a child and had fallen through the ice, he'd come to take her soul. She'd stopped him from drowning her. She'd held out her small hands and blocked his advances. She had changed his world that day. He'd watched her ever since. He'd taken drastic steps to make her vulnerable, to get her alone and manipulate events so that he could capture her.

6

The next morning Harmony fretted for hours about how to get home. The sound of knocking halted her thoughts. The fingernail she mindlessly chewed was pointy and uneven. She dropped her hand from her mouth and crossed the room to answer the door. Who else could she expect?

Suijin's broad shoulders filled the doorframe as he greeted her. The forced smile on her face was probably obvious to him, she thought, but she was going to be amiable long enough to ask him for his help getting home. Her herbs were gone. Maybe Suijin could retrieve the first ingredient from the sea serpent's cave.

"Come have breakfast with me." His cordial offer sounded more like a command.

Harmony nodded and followed him down the corridor. As the questions scrambled in her head, she tried to focus on remaining calm as she skimmed the tender flesh of her thumb over her jagged fingernail. They reached a large but cozy room with a marble hearth. A dining table supported various exotic fruits and a silver tray with sushi-like seafood. She narrowed in on a steaming pot, hoping it contained tea. Across from the table was a seating area where plush sofas rested on thick carpets, and beyond that was a colossal carved four-poster bed.

"Is this your bedroom?" Harmony asked, dazzled by the finery around her. These items had obviously come from the human realm.

Suijin chuckled. "Yes. I sleep here, eat here…I spend most of my time in this room when I'm indoors. It's comfortable here." He indicated the table. "Please, sit and eat. Have some tea."

After settling into a cushioned chair, she lifted a china tea cup and stared at the fine porcelain. He must have noticed her reaction.

"Over the centuries I've brought many items here from the human realm."

She wondered how he traveled to the other realm. *Does he use the herbs too?* she wondered. She reached for the teapot. She offered to pour a cup for him.

"I'd love some." He flashed a smiled.

Immediately she focused on the task at hand, pouring the tea without spilling it, while she fought the urge to steal a quick glance at him. He moved around the table and stood next to her chair. She had to crane her neck to get a thorough look. His extreme closeness made her uncomfortable. She set his cup in front of the vacant seat to her right, pushing it away as far as she could reach without being obvious.

"So how long are we going to visit? Maybe we could spend today together. After that you could suggest a way for me to cross the realms without my herbs." She practically guzzled her tea while she waited for his reply. The tea was hot and scorched her tongue. Feeling nervous under his intent gaze, she gave him a tight smile, wishing he wouldn't loom over her.

"I would enjoy spending the day with you, Harmony."

His long pause made her tap her foot in anticipation. She silently willed him to say the words she longed to hear. *Then I will take you home.*

He slid into the seat next to her and lifted the delicate teacup with his paw of a hand. He took a sip. Then he set the china down with grace and said, "If you are patient, I will take you back cross the realms—without the herbs."

Her eyes flew to his. Her audible exhale released her worries and fears. *Suijin can take me across.* She'd figured as much; after all, he was a god. Questions of what other miraculous things he was capable of hovered on the fringes of her mind. "Yes, I can be patient. Okay then, what shall we do today?" She reached for a peach and nibbled at the fruit while he made suggestions.

"We could go for a swim to the…" His words died on his lips when she shook her head and drew her brows together.

She gripped the delicate fruit in her palm, focusing on the fuzz. In a low voice, she quipped, "Funny thing. Something happened to me in the water when I was a child, and now I'm deathly afraid of it." He was the cause of her fear of deep water, a fact she not-so-subtly threw in his face. *Whoops!* She was supposed to be amiable—yet she couldn't keep her sarcastic, insinuating remark to herself. Regret tugged at her heart. *Just play his game, so you can go home.* She stuffed the peach into her big, sorry mouth.

"I understand. How thoughtless of me." He tipped his head and looked toward the ceiling as if searching for the answer there. He seemed to consider an idea. "We could take a stroll around the palace or around the city."

Harmony lifted a shoulder. "Okay." It took control not to drain her tea after she finished the peach. She wasn't hungry, but she wanted to appear aloof and polite. There was no way he was going to see her tremble as though she were the sacrificial lamb he would slaughter. She rose from the chair, indicating she was ready to move on with their day.

Just get through today.

Harmony trailed along beside him, listening to his history lessons about the palace and its vast contents. After viewing two dozen rooms, she expressed her appreciation for the great dining hall with its wall murals depicting sea life.

"Yes, they are lovely. They were painted by clan artisans centuries ago. Some were quite talented."

Binda's face came sharply into Harmony's mind. Her cousin had been a clan artist. Art was something the two girls had in common. Binda sketched designs used by the tribes as tattoo art while Harmony sketched architectural designs. Perhaps if Binda hadn't been killed, they could have become close—relatively close, as they would each live in different realms. Though Binda's death wasn't Harmony's fault directly, she still felt ultimately responsible. The walls seemed to be closing in as the old wounds reopened, exposing her guilt.

She shadowed Suijin into the next room where ornate porcelain and china were displayed. Vast and exquisitely furnished, the palace felt quiet and haunted. She and Suijin were alike—two shells with sad, haunting pasts. At the gallery window she beheld the ocean view. She noticed the road below and was suddenly desperate for fresh air.

"Can we go outside? I would like to walk around the town." Harmony spoke wistfully.

He joined her by the window and glanced out, perhaps to see what she was looking at. She scanned the broken roof of a building down the lane before she dared to glance up at him. When he swung his gaze to meet hers, her shoulders tensed. She thought the luminescent eyes of the Aquapopuleans were unusual and lovely, but they were nothing compared to Suijin's. The irises always changed colors. At this moment they appeared green and yellow, reminding Harmony of cats' eyes.

"Whatever you would like, Harmony," he murmured. He stood close and regarded her attentively.

Some of Suijin's raven hair hung over his shoulder and she noticed something was woven into the braid. She'd noticed it before. From up close, she saw that it was blond hair. She lifted the braid and held it up in the daylight.

"Is this blond hair?" Her hand flew to her own hair, a perfect match. That devastating day during the earthquake and tidal wave, Suijin had been in the water. The tidal wave had plucked her from the Wellness-by-the-Sea temple and deposited her in the bay. He had come after her—tried to take her. She'd used her ability and burned him to keep him away, but he had apparently managed to clip off a substantial lock of her hair.

"Jin, is this *my* hair?"

"I wanted a piece of you with me." His hand brushed hers, but she released the braid and drew back a fist. After a momentary stare-off, he added, "I also carry your brand." He pulled his loose, sleeveless tunic to the side, revealing puckered scars on his chest.

Her hand covered her mouth for a moment, her eyes wide. He released the fabric, again hiding his scarred skin.

"I did *that*?"

"Curious thing. I'm immortal, and I can heal my body of all wounds. Significant wounds take longer, but the scars from your burns have remained." His hand moved from his shirt to lift a cascade of her shining gold hair. He rolled the soft strands between his thumb and fingers. His irises blazed like the gilding on the china in the cases behind them. Softly he said, "You fascinate me, Harmony."

Instinctively she crossed her arms over her chest, one hand resting against her throat. Suddenly the ample room felt confining. She felt cornered, and her anger flared.

"You shouldn't take what doesn't belong to you. Those that play with fire get burned," she warned, sensing she'd aroused his interest another notch. She moved away from him, whipping the stands of hair from his fingers and over her shoulder. She marched toward the door, slowly realizing she didn't know the way through this maze of a palace. She clenched her teeth at his soft chuckle, forcing herself to regain control. *Play the game!* He easily overtook her lead, and they wordlessly made their way out into the sunshine.

As they explored the ancient city's housing district, she found she was watching him from lowered lashes. The sun was hot, and the glare off the stone street became too much. She left his side and stopped on the threshold of a dwelling. She could feel the dark coolness beckon her.

"Go ahead. The structure is sound." His voice was close behind her.

The entrance seemed typical of clan dwellings, though the rooms were sized more like her family home. Harmony paused by the window, which displayed a cinematic view of the palace above.

Suijin walked around looking at the surfaces with interest. Her eyes slid to rest on his broad back, and she wondered if he'd been lonely. Loneliness was a human trait. She recalled reading about people of status in her own world, kings and rock stars alike, all professing their loneliness because fame and fortune isolated them. She looked out the window again, up toward his remote palace.

"It's a shame the clans left this city. It seems like it would have been a lovely, productive place." She could understand why he resented them for leaving. She almost sympathized—almost.

"Yes. I'm an outcast once again." He sighed woefully.

Harmony speculated about his reference. He held her gaze with his long pause. Surely he was about to tell her what he meant. Instead he suggested, "Let's have a look upstairs." Then, he moved away in search of a staircase.

***

Standing at the top of the steps, Suijin listened to Harmony's footfalls ascending behind him. Without looking back, he turned down the hallway of the dwelling and wandered into sleeping quarters. A heavy iron bedframe dominated the room, its ironwork ornate, probably too heavy to move once it had been assembled. He placed his palm against the metal post.

He heard Harmony enter the room, walking slower now she'd caught up with him. He liked her chasing after him and wished it was for another reason. He knew he'd piqued her interest with his comment. Now he waited for her to start asking questions.

Her soft tone was laced with something other than curiosity though—was it concern?

"What did you mean about being outcast 'once again'?" she probed.

She stood at his shoulder, her face tilted up, and her eyes searched his. Her golden eyes were like the Aquapopuleans', yet distinctly human. *She is an extraordinary creature.*

"I existed long before life on this planet, far from these realms. There are other gods and goddesses who live among the stars."

He watched her blink rapidly, as if she were in a sandstorm, as she processed the otherworldly information. She silently waited for him to continue. "One such god sentenced me to this planet as punishment. I cannot leave these realms."

"Punishment?"

He knew he was already a villain in her eyes. He had taken away her loved ones and forced her to come here. Yet he decided to reveal his secret. "I was desired by the wife of a powerful, influential god. She pursued me. I made the wrong choice when I surrendered to her advances. When her husband discovered our affair, he hurled me into the oceans of the earthly realms—where I will remain for eternity."

"You were cast here because of a woman?" she said. Irony laced her tone, and she smirked.

He noted her point—he'd now taken *another* married woman who didn't belong to him. He imagined Harmony thought he deserved his punishment. Gods generally didn't justify their actions, but he wanted to be clear. "That goddess was out of his control. I was but one of her many conquests. I was young, called a yearling by the other gods, even though I was a million years old when she seduced me. Anyway, it wasn't the fact that she had lovers that bothered her husband—gods have many lovers—but he overheard her telling me that she loved me. When gods pledge their love to their mates it is infinite. She devastated him. Out of anger, he unjustly locked me here on this small speck in the universe."

"Humph. I thought there was only one god. I thought you were it."

"I am merely one of thousands. And I'm the son of gods less powerful than those who rule the universe," he said humbly.

"There's no one who'd help you return like your parents? Friends…the wife? Did you…do you return her love?" He heard the hesitation in her voice when she asked if he'd loved the goddess. Did she find it interesting that he had been desired by a powerful goddess?

"No one would rebuke *his* authority," Suijin stated with finality. "Besides, godly parents are nothing like human parents. Nurturing is an abstract concept. The one good thing about being restricted to the earthy realms is I've learned about affection, devotion, and I've seen people sacrifice for their loved ones. I've studied mankind since they evolved. After all this time, I've finally learned what true love is. And I did not love the goddess." With his finger, he traced a pattern carved into the metal bedframe. He yearned to tell Harmony that he'd loved her from the moment he'd seen her. Even though she was only a small girl, she'd made a big impression.

"Jin?"

"Mmm," he mumbled, looking at but not seeing the pattern he traced.

"You know what it's like to be a prisoner," Harmony said, and then she sighed for emphasis.

Her words affected him grievously. Abruptly turning to her, he said, "No! Don't think of yourself as my prisoner. I will give you anything to make you happy here—if you only give me the chance."

She gripped the opposite bedpost. "I want to go home. I don't understand why you think there could be anything between us."

Slowly advancing toward her, he ran his palm along the footboard rail. "I know you feel something for me. I know you are confused. There has been turmoil and tragedy in your life, but the time has come for you to put it all behind you. I can give you so much...if only you'd open yourself to me. Don't hold back, Harmony."

"I'm married," she said flatly.

"Only just. And he has left you." He knew his words stung her from the way she blanched, but in pointing out the truth he hoped she'd see reason.

"Even if Kodiak didn't come back from the expedition—which he will—you think I'd come running to you?" She snorted. "That's ridiculous!"

"I want you to kiss me. Kiss me and see what you feel for me," he challenged.

They again locked in a stare-off.

7

Harmony felt frustration build. *Who does he think he is? Just because he was desired by a goddess doesn't mean I desire him.* She glared at him but was abruptly caught off guard as his irises changed; the violet hue now chased out the gold streaks. Her ire slipped, and she wondered, *Where has he gotten this ludicrous notion that I have feelings for him? How absurd! His kiss won't be magical. I won't fall under his spell. And I'll prove it to him!*

"Harmony, I—"

Perhaps he meant to apologize for his crude way of loving her, but she stepped forward to place her hands on the thick trunks of his arms. He seemed surprised, and she'd felt gratification in that. She watched the color in his irises deepen, drawing her in like quicksand. She inhaled a quick breath into her tight lungs. Her nostrils flared and filled with the scent of his skin. When he lowered his willing mouth to hers, their lips brushed.

A cosmic heatwave pulsed through her. As her hot mouth fused with his, he wrapped his arms around her slender body and kissed her back with fervor. She'd meant to prove that his kiss made her feel nothing, but she was dead wrong! That moment when she could tell herself she felt nothing eluded her. On the contrary…

His mouth had been open mid-sentence, and she tasted him straight away. Her tongue swept inside the opening, ruthlessly giving him a sample of what he could *never* have, but fate played a cruel trick when she experienced the most exotic taste ever. It sent tiny shivers all over her flesh. She completely forgot what she was trying to accomplish while her tongue plunged for more. His arms locked around her waist, lifting her closer. She teetered on her tippy toes. Her hands gripped his biceps, and she clutched him tighter. Her heart pounded before she dropped her head back for a breath. Suijin kissed the corner of her mouth, then her chin, and he recaptured her lips. She wrapped her arms around his neck, pulling him closer. He groaned deep in the back of his throat—she felt its force vibrate into her mouth and spread down and across her chest. His firm lips meshed with hers, snug and perfect.

Her conscious mind screamed for her to stop. It suddenly felt like something was squeezing her brain. *I must stop before I am lost. Damn, I need my ability to stop him! He must be making me feel this way!*

Her eyes opened halfway, her lids heavy. Their noses still touched, as did their lips. She felt their breath mingle. Her arms slightly loosened from his neck, and she slid a hand into his hair to cradle the back of his head. He didn't take the kisses any deeper as he loosened his hold, but he didn't let her go. She realized his tongue had never searched hers out, never crossed into her territory; it just met hers as she explored. She'd been the aggressor.

Her eyes flew wide open to look at him. Their brows nearly touching, she waited until his eyes fluttered open. When they did, he regarded her without judgement. She watched his irises swirl like gray smoke. She couldn't pull her mouth from his, even now. He was intoxicating.

Clutching a fistful of his dark hair, she drew her hand back from his head and tugged until his mouth left hers. She was rougher than she needed to be, and he winced. Her chin inches from his, she waited for her heart to stop thudding so hard.

Her heavy panting fanned his face, and they continued to regard one another. Harmony knew he was waiting for her to make the next move. She cursed her tense, aroused body. An overwhelming guilt surged through her, followed by irrational anger.

"You beast!" she hissed through clenched teeth. "Why are you doing this?" She yanked hard on his hair again. She sent him a menacing look. "Stay out of my head. Don't make me feel things that aren't real."

"I haven't," he protested. He released a sigh at her accusation. "Harmony, I won't do that. I want you to want me all on your own."

"You're lying!" Yet she was reluctant to let him go. A sincere smile tugged the corners of his mouth, and his eyes softened. The gray smoke swirled away, leaving a blueish hue in their wake. She'd never seen his eyes turn blue. It was as if storm clouds had rolled away to leave the twilight sky exposed, beautiful and clear.

They both realized what she was feeling was real...and raw. Harmony released her hold on his hair and slipped her hand from the silky strands. Desperately she wiggled free from his arms. He let her slip away. She observed his enthusiastic smile, sensed his smugness.

But the discovery of something between them she'd never thought possible cost her. She comprehended the enormous risk involved in remaining here with him.

No! I don't feel anything for him! she screamed in her mind. *He must have tricked me somehow. I must get home soon!* She backed away, waiting for him to pursue her, to persuade her to return to his arms, but he only watched. As much as she wanted to believe he'd made her feel false feelings she knew she it was a lie; guilt very nearly choked her. She loved Kodi—not this beast! *How can I feel like this?*

"I promise you, Harmony, I will love and cherish you for many lifetimes. I can prolong your life. We will be happy together. Just allow me to show you pleasure. I will only give it to you if you ask. Just ask."

"I don't want your promises!" The back of her hand pressed against her lips to stop the lingering tingle. "I'm going back." When she reached the doorframe, she turned back and yelled, "Don't follow me!" Her voice cracked, and she shook with rage. Blinded by tears, she spun and ran down the hallway.

***

Now Suijin knew that Harmony felt something for him, not a fleeting something but a feeling ignited by carnal desire. He saw that desire dissipate when anger flashed like torches in her fiery eyes. When she finally spoke he hadn't been disheartened. After all, actions speak louder than words.

8

Suijin left the dwelling and turned to follow the road that led to the sea. Being away from the water too long made him rambunctious. Immediately when his torso hit the waves he transformed himself back into a god. The scales that ran down his outer arms and thighs returned. His inner temple was restored.

His mind was occupied with thoughts of the woman within his grasp; Harmony Parker would be his at last. He needed this quiet time to assess what had just happened between them and to gauge how to proceed. But he sensed he was not alone. A siren trailed at a distance. He could dive deep and lose her; he knew she would have to surface for air after thirty minutes, but he swam toward the light. When he broke the surface, she did too.

"Jin." Luna's voice was high and pleasant but disappointed. "Why have you brought her here? I am not enough for you?"

Yesterday he'd asked Luna to prepare a room for an esteemed guest, but he'd avoided answering her questions so he could get back to Harmony, who he'd left on the beach.

"You are immensely important to me, but you are a siren. I seek other companionship. You know I covet you above all the other sirens. Be content with that." Suijin's black eyes watched her effortlessly tread water. "Harmony Parker is my destiny…what I've waited the millennium for. I must make her feel welcome. She is my heart and desire." He glided to Luna, his hands clasping her cold cheeks. His hands were so large against her small skull that only her eyes peeked through them. "Luna, you must help me by making Harmony comfortable. I'm counting on you, my dearest one." After a moment, he felt her head nod in his hands. Her eyes closed, and he brushed a kiss across her mouth.

Suijin released the siren and slipped soundlessly underwater. To burn off his restless energy, he swam around the continents during the next hour. Ready to return to his beloved, he vowed he would make her understand that she was different and her potential was limitless. Maybe he could persuade her just a little.

He entered the city and walked up the curving hill to the palace, all the while cursing his decision to become man-like. After the invigorating swim as himself, he felt like he was wearing a confining suit that was too small for him. Reaching the summit, he found Harmony pacing at the palace entrance.

She stopped and faced him. "What do you want from me?"

Hmm, she is still angry. He paused several strides away, his stance casting a long shadow beneath the afternoon sun.

She is so beautiful.

It was easy to be distracted by her appearance. Harmony's wavy blond hair drifted on the constant breeze. Her long, shapely limbs were ridged with attitude, her shoulders back, chest heaving, chin jutting. Her defiance only made him desire her more. He stated his truth: "I want your devotion. I want you to know me and be with me." He was stimulated by the angry sparkle in her amber eyes; her lack of fear sent a chill through him. Had he finally met his match? "I will give you what you need while you are a guest in my palace."

"Guest!" She choked on an ironic laugh. "I have been here too long! I want to go home."

"I see you need some time to get used to this idea, so I'll leave you to think about your options." He moved past her but stopped at the door. His offer was sincere.

"You are free to explore the palace, the village, and all around the island. But know this—escape is impossible. This is a deserted place, with only sirens to keep you company."

"I won't let those things near me."

He inhaled, mulling a thought while his eyes washed over her tense form. A muscle flexed in his jaw. "Yes, I've felt what you've done to my girls in the past." Deep in the recesses of his mind, he'd sensed the torture they'd experienced from Harmony's burns.

She raised her chin a notch, rebellious. "Your 'girls'," she repeated sarcastically.

He realized that her comment and smirk were intended to annoy him. She was testing him by reminding him that he wasn't the only one with powers. She was cognizant of the power she held over him. In his true form, if he could somehow push past her defense shield and she touched him, she would burn his skin. She could make him suffer, and she would; he had no doubt. But his concern right now was for the sirens.

"They will not harm you, Harmony. Don't hurt them," he warned." The growl in his voice reached its target. Undeterred, Harmony arched an eyebrow at his cautionary threat. He turned away swiftly and entered the palace without a backward glance. He had to fight the urge to release a frustrated laugh.

***

After the kiss, everything changed. She wasn't going to play nice or oblige him in any way. After spending twenty-four hours with him, she knew all she wanted to know about him. Now she wanted to go home.

He'd made it clear he wasn't ready for her to go.

For the next two weeks she gave him the cold shoulder, not uttering a word more than she had to and turning her back to him at every opportunity. During that time she scouted out every room and every crevice on the island, to no avail. There was nothing she could use as a boat to get away. There were no herbs to send her back. Nothing.

Every morning, food was laid out on the kitchen counter, an amazing variety of breads and fruits. It was replaced throughout the day with other delectable food to nibble on. That was fine with her, as long as he kept his distance. She would force him to realize she was not interested in him. But she wondered what he did all day.

Curious, she watched him one morning. He met a siren at the dock, where a massive stone staircase began on dry land and then submerged underwater. The siren floated a basket filled with goods to the edge of the steps. Suijin walked down the expansive stairs that descended into the ocean, stopping waist deep. The girl standing beside him handed over the basket, and he set it safely on the nearby stone ledge. He turned his attention back to the girl, who grinned up at him. His hands slipped under the water to grab her waist. Pulling her toward his bare chest, he gave her a thorough kiss of thanks that made Harmony cast her intruding eyes away. When she dared look again he was trudging up the steps, the basket on his hip. The siren floated on her back, watching him.

Later that evening Harmony stood by his bedroom door. Each evening, Suijin prepared and cooked some delicacy from the sea in the fireplace. Harmony wondered what it was like in times past when the Aquapopuleans had occupied these very rooms. It was her only cooked meal each day, and she started showing up after only four evenings. It was time to give in, as far as food was concerned. When he tried to have a conversation, she kept her responses minimal, and she excused herself the moment she was finished eating. But loneliness was setting in. *Maybe I'll just talk to him for a few minutes*, she thought. *Otherwise I'll go crazy.*

When he sat the plate before her, she murmured, "Thank you. This smells wonderful."

He remained silent. She forced her eyes to his face. When their eyes met he nodded before he turned to take his seat.

So he isn't talking now?

Harmony understood loneliness, and she wondered again if Suijin felt lonely in this place. He'd mentioned other sirens besides Luna, but she'd only seen the one giving him the basket. The one he'd kissed.

"Are there many sirens in the waters around this island? I've only seen one." Harmony kept her eyes down and picked at the fish on her plate.

Suijin drummed a finger on the table until she looked up at him. "They know you are here and are too afraid to come close to shore."

She felt her cheeks heat. Killing another breathing creature didn't sit well with Harmony—even though the siren had attacked her. "I did what I had to." Her voice was hollow. Harmony remembered what the human-like sirens were capable of. "The sirens are foul creatures. When I was with the clans and the tribes, I heard that the sirens lured their loved ones into the water to certain death. Why did you send them to do such things?"

Suijin gave her an odd look. "I did not send them," he objected. "The sirens have their own minds." Agitated, he began drumming his finger again. "I don't deny what they do in this realm or in the human realm, but they have remained loyal to me."

"Sirens are in the human realm?" She sputtered, nearly choking on the bite of fish she'd just swallowed.

His white teeth flashed at her surprise. He clarified. "From time to time throughout history, sirens have followed me through the portal. In your human folklore since early man, they were called mermaids."

"Oh." Harmony wanted to say, *Wow, that's weird*, but her whole life was weird now. What else could really surprise her?

"Of course, once I realized what they were doing—drowning sailors—I made them return to this realm. I'm much better at keeping the balance now."

Her meal forgotten, she leaned forward, engaged in the conversation. "If you didn't send them, maybe you should tell the Aquapopuleans. Maybe you could persuade the sirens to stop terrorizing those people." Many of "those people" were her friends and family.

"Why should I?" He sniffed. "I tried to nurture the clans while I lived among them, but they wanted me to remain...untouchable. And I never asked for their worship. After I lost my love for that species, I sought humans for companionship. The humans had already invented their own gods, which, I suppose, left me worse off than the Aquapopuleans had." He shook his dark head and slouched back in his chair. "Their fate is no different from any other mortals."

"So the sirens offered you companionship?" Harmony supposed he meant in a carnal way.

"Some sirens have kept me company throughout this endless life. I extended the lives of two sirens, but even the sirens die. I cannot make them immortal. They naturally live as long as the Aquapopuleans, about one hundred and forty years. I lived here with Sirena for a thousand years. After Sirena I found Luna. Both their songs stirred me. The melodies made me feel emotions I haven't felt in millions of years. Luna has the same vocal gift as Sirena."

Harmony watched his gaze wander off as he spoke lovingly of the sirens Sirena and Luna. When his gaze returned to hers, he said, "How can I express to you that you too make me feel…something I have never before felt? If you accept me, I have the power to make you immortal, but you have to want me as your eternal mate."

His words begged for her compassion, but Harmony wasn't willing to see him as someone who deserved her empathy. She would never see herself as his eternal mate—as oddly flattering as the notion was. She loved another.

She rose to leave. They were done talking as far as she was concerned. Her changes of expression, from curious to understanding and then resolve to hate him, were broadcast across her lovely face.

"Goodnight," she said resolutely.

Suijin simply nodded, perhaps not wanting to give her cause for anger.

9

Harmony strolled across the field and up the hill to the apple orchard, the ancient city at her back. She pondered which apple varieties were ready for harvest here in early October; the apples appeared ripe for picking. She'd made no mistake when she calculated she had been here for nearly three weeks. Suijin's promise to bring her home had been a lie. It was beyond frustrating that she couldn't get through to him. Pausing to take a cleansing breath of mingled ocean and orchard air, she sighed. The apple trees reminded her of home. She recalled her favorite orchard in Hampton Falls, where her family went for years to pick their favorites for making pie.

Home. Her heart longed to return. *Kodiak must be so concerned...confused. What can he be thinking?*

The sweet scent comforted her, and the bees that buzzed past her ears where too busy to bother with her. She left the orchard and walked to the beach where Suijin had delivered her by boat. She shielded her eyes, checking to see if maybe the boat had washed ashore.

She noticed something in the water. But it was small and darker than the navy ocean. A girl's head broke the surface.

A siren.

The girl must have touched bottom, because she stood with her shoulders above the blanket of sparkling waves. She made slow but steady progress toward the shore. Harmony backed up a few steps, though she stood several feet from where the waves broke. *Sirens don't venture out of the water.*

But this one did.

The siren walked onto the sand as if she were human.

56

The dark-haired girl had a juvenile look and oversized eyes—telltale features of a siren.

Unintentionally, heat surged down Harmony's arms, and her palms felt as though they were buzzing. Suijin said the sirens were afraid of her, but this one wasn't. In fact, her evil stare was anything but frightened.

"What do you want?" Harmony barked, hoping she would leave.

"I am Luna. Suijin sent me to find you and ask that you return to the palace." Her sweet voice belied her expression of hatred.

Luna's hair was as black as squid ink, her skin as white as the midnight moon, her eyes the color of the darkest blue sea. And her voice was as hauntingly beautiful as she was. Her melancholy lyrics had ensnared the god. Probably anyone who heard her was instantly mesmerized.

Harmony remembered what Suijin had said about Luna and Sirena, the sirens he seemed to care greatly about. Now she recalled that he had mentioned they could walk on land.

"You live in the palace?"

Luna pulled her long black hair to one side and began to squeeze away the excess water. She took her time answering Harmony. "Yes. Suijin has bestowed this gift upon me so I can live with him in his palace...as he did for the siren before me."

"Sirena?"

Luna's back straightened further. "Sirena was Suijin's first companion. He swam the oceans for many years to the comforting sound of whales' songs, but he longed for intimate companionship." Luna's dainty legs moved up the beach, leaving child-sized footprints in the sand. She paused, looking expectantly over her shoulder at Harmony.

Harmony obligingly followed when Luna resumed

both her steps and her tale. "Over time nature took its course. Homo sapiens further developed along the water's protective edge. Aquapopulo and humans alike advanced. You see, at the time he first arrived in the earthly realms, life was just beginning to evolve. Suijin loved and coveted the ones that formed in his image. He nurtured them in the water, both Aquapopuleans and sirens, leaving the humans to their own devices. Eventually the Aquapopulean's inquisitive nature drove them onto the land, and soon they worshiped him in another way."

Luna sneered, confirming her intense dislike of the Aquapopuleans.

"In the meantime, our kind stayed in the water. We used the Aquapopulean men to populate the oceans with more female sirens. Procreating with and then taking their men to their deaths hasn't helped our reputation," she said with a smirk.

Harmony shuddered inwardly. She believed the sirens were devious creatures, and this admission solidified her reservations. She pondered Luna's relationship with Suijin.

They wandered through the orchard silently for some time until Harmony inquired, "So how long have you and Suijin been together?"

"More than two centuries," she said smugly without breaking her stride.

Harmony sensed Luna's confidence when it came to whom she coveted. "That's a long time. He's given you quite a gift, the ability to walk on land and live in his palace. It sounds like you're his wife?"

Luna's eyes narrowed and she cut her gaze to Harmony, who stood more than a foot taller than her. "You would think so. However, in Suijin's eyes I'm merely a siren. Apparently, he desires something else."

The two women were silent, emotions running high.

"Look, Luna, I didn't ask to come here. Suijin gave me no choice. He's promised I can go home after I get to know him." Harmony's arms flew up to emphasize her distress. "But who knows how long he's thinking of keeping me here. I want to go home, to return to the human realm."

The city came into view beyond the field they'd entered. Luna turned her gaze to the tall grasses. Her placid expression made Harmony wonder what this girl knew and wasn't saying.

"Do you know his intentions? Do you think he will let me go? Luna, please!"

"Suijin will decide what he wants and when he wants it, human," the siren said with force.

Harmony wanted to scream. She no longer felt—human. She was an anomaly, feasibly a creature similar to this siren.

"I know you don't want me here anymore than I want to be here." Harmony read her acknowledgement in the siren's face. Encouraged, she went on. "You could talk to him. Persuade him to return me to my realm."

"He will be angry with me if I say that."

"But wouldn't it be worth the risk? You love him, don't you? You could have him all to yourself again." Harmony watched the emotions play across Luna's youthful face. "I've been here for weeks—I need to go home."

"Yes, I know how long you've been here, human. He's had me stay away all this time so you could get used to him and this island. Don't you think him sending me to get you today signals that he wants us to get to know one another?"

"Do you want to get to know me, Luna?" Harmony raised her brows in doubt.

The siren abruptly stopped and swiveled her head in Harmony's direction. She said icily, "I wish he'd drowned you along with the rest of your family."

Harmony was stunned by the ruthless remark. Luna made it completely clear that she didn't want Harmony there. She felt ribbons of heat snake down her arms. She could burn this insolent bitch if she desired, but the hurtful words revealed Luna's true jealousy, and Harmony, on some level, accepted that. The heat dissipated as Luna walked away. Harmony didn't retort. She followed Suijin's chosen siren back to the palace in silence.

***

The next several weeks were difficult for Luna. Suijin seemed obsessed with the human, to the point of adjusting the currents to bring warmer waters and winds to keep her comfortable. He instructed Luna to gather varieties of food to keep her fed. Wanting trinkets to gift her, he sent the siren into the human realm to retrieve items while he tried to woo a woman who claimed she didn't want him. But Luna knew differently. She'd watched them together—and it was ripping her heart apart.

For the third consecutive night, Harmony refused to dine with Suijin. He sent Luna to her room with a plate of food. She knocked quietly.

"Go away!"

"I have your dinner." Luna's voice was flat and tight.

Harmony opened the door and raised a curious brow. "You could have left it, like the others. What do you want?"

Luna had been leaving Harmony's dinner trays outside her door the past nights. Although Suijin remained patient with his guest, he'd asked Luna to care for her and get her whatever luxuries she desired. Luna was fed up. Not only was this human coming between her and Suijin in the social sense, but the physical sense too. He'd not mated with her or any sirens since Harmony had crossed the realm months ago. Luna glared at her. "Suijin sent this for you." She lifted the plate, filled with an assortment of tasty items. "But you don't deserve it."

Harmony pleaded her case again. "He is keeping me here against my will. I don't want to be here anymore than you want me here, Luna."

"Ha!" The sound was raspy, and Luna's narrow chin jutted. "I see the way you look at him. You think he doesn't know how you watch him." She bared her pearly teeth. "Everyone wants him! But he is mine! I will never let him make you his wife."

"Wait! What?" Harmony looked confused. "Wife? He wants to make me his wife? He spoke of love and companionship—but I thought he just wanted to have me as a conquest or something."

"Bedding you is not a cure for his infatuation. He loves you, and he will never let you leave. Only death will release you." Luna dropped the silver tray. It clattered upon impact. The ceramic plate hit the stones and smashed, and Harmony jumped back to avoid being splashed by the contents.

Luna swirled away and marched down the hallway. She hoped Harmony would starve to death.

10

Days later when Harmony entered her room, she wondered for the hundredth time if she could she get Luna to help her escape. It seemed plausible. She would have to think of a way to persuade her.

Suijin continued to leave her gifts each day: soaps, garments, trinkets, and flowers. Today, it looked like he had left her something else. A large steamer trunk had been placed at the end of her bed. Curious, she bent down and unhinged the latches. She raised the heavy lid and lifted her hand to her mouth, shocked.

These are my things!

Reaching into the trunk, she pulled out article after article of clothing that had been hanging in her closet or folded in drawers in her New Castle bedroom. Strewn across the bed were her pink robe, her jeans and tee-shirts, several bikinis. Other familiar fabrics in the trunk caught her eye. Digging around she discovered her hairbrush, toothbrush, makeup, and shoes.

"What the hell! I'm not moving in!" she hollered aloud.

Though she was glad to wear her own clothes and use her own things, she was still annoyed with Suijin. He'd gone into her house, through her personal items. Had Kodiak been there? If not, would he notice her clothes were suddenly missing from the hangers? Her toothbrush from the sink? What if Samantha's father or some other neighbor had seen Suijin?

She dressed and left to meet him for dinner. She would have a lot to say tonight.

When Harmony entered the room, she could smell fish cooking. She spotted a new item on table, a decanter of wine. *Some liquid courage might be just the thing to support my upcoming tirade*, she thought. But the future scolding seemed to fade for the moment. She said, "Wow, where did this come from?"

Suijin strolled over and stood next to her. Lifting the empty bottle, he turned it to reveal the label. "I sent Luna to the otherworld to retrieve it for you."

She looked up at him in shock; it was her favorite brand of red. Immediately his nearness overwhelmed her, and she shuffled back several steps. "Oh? Did she also bring over my personal things?" Had he sent the sneaky siren into her home?

He grinned at her and then cast his gaze along her torso, seeming to admire the sundress she wore. "Yes, I instructed Luna to do so. I wanted you to be more comfortable here. I want this palace to feel like your home."

"I'm not staying here. You said just for a while..." Her words trailed off when she watched his dismissive expression.

"We have plenty of time." He poured her a glass of wine. "Have some and relax. Tonight we will get to know each other better. Then we will see what tomorrow brings."

"I want to go home tomorrow," she insisted.

He raised an eyebrow, his grin still in place. "Drink up."

She considered refusing, but she was already miserable from being away from her home, and the wine *was* her favorite. Just one glass would relax her, and maybe she'd finally get a full night's sleep. Harmony accepted the glass and took a hearty gulp. She turned away and roamed the room, thinking, *Fine! I'll get through this evening—but that's it!*

"So what's with your siren, Luna? She says she's been with you a long time."

"Yes," he confirmed as he filled their plates with fish and sautéed greens.

"Will she be joining us then?" She made a show of glancing around; quite sure Luna wouldn't be making an appearance.

"It's just us tonight." He indicated a chair. "Sit. Eat something."

She acknowledged it was kind of Suijin to cook for her. She took another sip and savored the wine, a small comfort from home, before she sat. After a few more sips she thanked him for the meal and the wine. While she ate she listened to his voice as he told her about the evolution of early human society, but she found his explanation too abstract to follow. Trying to concentrate on what he was saying, instead she found herself focused on his eyes. *What color are they, exactly?*

She felt strange, tranquil. Her heavy eyelids slipped closed. When she opened her eyes again, she was lying back against an array of pillows.

How did I get here? Did I fall asleep at dinner?

She felt overheated and lifted her heavy hair off her shoulders, casting it over the pillows.

"Are you comfortable?" Suijin sat next to her, his arm flung across the upholstery.

"I'm warm." Her voice sounded far-off. Her fingertips slid the soft fabric of her dress up over her thighs, allowing more airflow. But then she felt his strong hand on her knee. It moved up her bare skin. She inhaled at the sensation. It felt nice. Relaxing more deeply, she wondered, *How did I get here? What was I thinking about? Oh yeah, Suijin's eyes. I was thinking about his eyes!* They reflected in the firelight like pewter. His lashes were coal black. Part of his hair was drawn up in a knot at the crown of his head, and the rest flowed dark and free to his shoulders. She saw his generous lips move, but what had he asked?

"I'm warm," she said again, answering randomly. She pulled uselessly at the strap of her garment, exposing her collarbone when the fabric slipped from her satin skin.

Suijin scooted closer to her. She hadn't removed his hand from her thigh, and it wandered higher. "I will cool you." He leaned in and blew gently on her neck. The cool blast sent a river of shivers down her spine. Her mouth opened with a sharp breath. He moved his lips closer to hers.

She was oddly transfixed by him. Somewhere a warning sounded in her mind, screaming that he was off limits, forbidden. But that very thought—taking something that was forbidden—made her heart pound faster. His dark head, only inches from hers, dipped down, and she inhaled the fresh scent of his hair. He placed a gentle kiss just below the hollow of her throat, and then he snaked his tongue along her collarbone. Her breath caught. He swiveled his smiling lips to meet hers and waited.

Her fingers itched to loosen the knot that held back his hair. It was as if they had a mind of their own when they reached out and tugged the string until his dark wavy hair framed his face. The corners of his mouth turned up. Her eyes, the pupils enlarged, roved over his face before she reached for him, skimming her palm across his jaw and locking her fingers behind his neck.

***

He willed his hand to move slowly over her thigh; her eyes widened at his touch. As her dilated eyes focused on him, he understood the drug was working. This was what he wanted to see. This was the flame he'd lit. He'd dreamed of this moment so often. But he'd manipulated her, deceived her. He'd drugged her. He could have physically taken what he wanted from her, but he was afraid that wouldn't be enough. He wanted her to feel this way about him for real. He wanted her to want him.

Still, he needed a taste of her. Something to reward his patience. He was a god, after all.

His lips brushed hers, and he felt a wave wash over him. What she did to him was unlike anything he'd known. She pressed her mouth closer, arching her back. He captured her mouth, and she urged him on. Their breathless kisses left their mouths open for plunder, and she thrust her warm tongue into his. A second wave washed over him. These were unfamiliar feelings. These were the waves of desire he'd been waiting to experience. He'd known she was the one to spend eternity with. He pressed her back against the pillows. She wove her fingers tighter in his hair.

Although her ability to burn his skin with her touch was useless because he'd assumed this man-like form, when her hands slid free from his silky locks and she rubbed her palms against his hard chest and broad shoulders, he was tortured in another way. He didn't want her only this time! And he didn't want to drug her every time he needed her touch. He knew he couldn't let tonight go any further or she'd never come to truly love him. He just needed a taste, a promise of what was to come...

He withdrew his hand from under her dress, where it had wandered to intimate places. He sat back and pulled her roaming hands from his skin. Her arms strained to resume their exploration. He covered her hands with his on her lap, holding them in place. His breath was long and ragged as he watched her eyes plead with his.

He stood. "It's late. Time for you to rest." He stepped to the open window, drawing on the ocean's strength. Why he needed strength to protect him from one mere woman boggled his mind. Lost in his thoughts, he didn't hear her approach behind him. She wrapped her arms around his waist, and he felt her bare breasts press against his back.

Argh! He was angry with himself. He had done this underhandedly to sample what he would inevitably have, but it was backfiring. He was the one being tested. When he turned, she stepped back to offer him a look at what she offered. He bit his lower lip and drew blood. One step brought them together again. He ran his fingertip over her delicately arched brow. She was perfect. He swept her into his arms and carried her to her room. Along the way she licked and kissed his neck and sucked on his earlobe. Gently, he set her on the bed and stood back. "Not tonight, my love." He bent and gave her a chaste kiss before he left her lying naked and alone, yearning for him.

11

The next morning over breakfast, Harmony eyed Suijin from under her lashes. In the past, the water god had haunted her nightmares filled with drownings. But last night, she'd had the strangest dream about him—a vivid erotic dream. Her cheeks warmed even now just thinking about it. His mouth had been all over her, and she craved him. His hands had squeezed and pawed, and she'd woken entangled in damp sheets. She licked her lips, remembering the taste of him. The day she had kissed him in the city house flashed across her mind. Though she'd denied she liked it or had any feelings for him, she'd apparently enjoyed his kiss subconsciously entirely too much. She fixed her eyes on his mouth while he sucked on juicy cantaloupe before he popped the fruit into his mouth. She was momentarily mesmerized.

I want to taste his mouth right now! No—damn it! She dropped her eyes to her plate. These visions left her with guilty feelings. She was a married woman. She loved Kodiak. So why would she dream of her captor, the very person who'd taken her away from Kodiak and her home?

"Would you like to explore the seas with me this morning?" Suijin asked her, jolting her from her thoughts. "I can image you are restless with nothing to do all day."

Indeed she was! "I want to go home."

"Not yet. You've just arrived. You must give us time to know each other better, Harmony. You agreed."

Harmony pulled her mouth tight and snipped, "Do you have a boat?"

He frowned, rubbing his palms together. "I will fetch one. And then I will take you to an island that has volcanic mud. The mud is good for the skin. The sirens love it, and so do I. Would you like to try it?"

"All right, I'll go with you—if you get a boat." She crossed her arms over her chest. Any hunger she felt evaporated.

The fear of deep water was rooted in her past, and she hated that it had a crippling power over her. The water god was likely the safest entity to be in the water with—as long as he wasn't trying to kill her, which they'd established he wasn't. If only her powers could dissolve her fears and insecurities, she would embrace them. However, her ability seemed to only cause destruction to sirens and sea serpents. What good did that do? She originally thought she wanted to bury these talents, but they gave her an edge. However, she feared it was an edge toward the dark side. She wasn't yet willing to open that door—even though something about it was gratifying.

When they arrived at the volcanic island Harmony sat up in the tiny boat. Suijin had propelled the boat there with blurring speed while she lay down and closed her eyes. She was dressed in her own bikini, thanks to Luna. Now, holding her floppy hat against the wind, Harmony absorbed the incredible view. The mountains soared. The majority of the island was covered in tropical growth. A large waterfall fed a river that cascaded to the sea. Its banks were gray with clay.

Suijin dragged the boat on the shore and helped Harmony out.

"Wow, this island is beautiful."

"Mmm," he rumbled. "Wait until you feel the mud on your skin."

He clasped her hand, leading the way. Harmony was about to slip her hand from his, but she hesitated. It made her feel oddly secure...and wanted. His grin and his excitement over mud made her want to laugh. She tried not to let his lightheartedness penetrate her wall of indifference. The smile that played on her lips was all the emotion she planned to reveal.

They reached an area near the bank where they could enter the muddy water. She flexed her feet in the cool squishy mud that oozed between her toes. It was softer than the sand at Hampton Beach near her hometown. Releasing his hand, she stepped in, dipping her toe in to test the water temperature. "Wow! It's surprisingly warm." Just as she turned to ask what they did now, a clump of mud hit the middle of her back. Startled and shivering with gooseflesh, she stared open-mouthed at Suijin.

"Hey!" she cried indignantly. Then another cool mud splat hit her abdomen. "Jin! Stop that!"

"I just wanted you to get accustomed to the mud." He shrugged, pretending innocence.

"Oh yeah?" She bent over and wiggled her fingers down in the wet clay, grasping a clump. When she stood and launched it at him, he easily dodged it. She was quick to hurl another scoop, but again he twisted, and the mud landed by his bare foot. He sauntered toward her with a playful gleam in his eyes. She found herself wondering what color his eyes would be now and held her breath as he stepped closer to her. She slapped her hand, still caked in clay, on his chest, leaving a cartoon handprint.

"Ha! I got you." She chuckled.

Harmony sought the ever-changing pigment in his amused eyes to quench her curiosity. Her heart nearly stopped when she saw that his irises closely matched the copper color of Kodiak's. Her humor and smile faded.

"Mmm." He nodded, inspecting her artwork. "Can you do my back?"

"I don't think so," she mumbled, turning her head to scout out an escape.

"But if you do not help me, then I must call upon my sirens for assistance."

His teasing was met with a harsh retort. "I don't care what you do."

But she did! The thought of sirens nearby her made her nervous. And the thought of rubbing mud onto his skin made her hot and bothered! It wasn't right—she loved Kodiak, so she put that wall up higher as she stepped away from Suijin. It was impossible to look at him with those eyes. "I just want to relax," she said over her shoulder while she stepped up next to a leggy shrub.

His sigh was heavy, but he didn't ask her what had suddenly changed.

She acted like she didn't have a care in the world, like this was a typical spa day. Flinging her floppy hat onto the nearby bush, she was satisfied it wouldn't get mud on it; nor would the wind lift it from the spiky surface. The tips of her wavy hair, which reached the middle of her back, were covered in mud, thanks to Suijin. She shook her hair out before twisting and securing the windblown mane on her head with a hair tie. She knelt and began applying mud to her arms. He dropped to his knees next to her.

Out of her corner of her eye, she watched Suijin apply the mud. The cake that landed on her belly had fallen to the ground so she added more, running her finger down to the edges of her hot pink bikini bottoms.

"The mud may discolor the fabric. You should take it off."

Her head whipped around and she hissed, "You wish!" But once she saw him, her laughter couldn't be contained. She giggled. "You look ridiculous!"

Suijin had painted wavy lines across his face and torso and swirled lines around his pecs. He seemed pleased to have lightened her mood.

Harmony returned to her task and applied mud to her own body as Suijin watched her. The thick material felt smooth and cool on her sun-kissed skin. Suijin spoke about the uninhabited volcanic island. In the human realm birds would have found their way to this paradise, but flying birds hadn't evolved in this realm. He explained that this peaceful location drew the sirens and sometimes their young.

"Baby sirens?" Harmony pondered on the subject. She remarked, "I've only seen female sirens, and they've all looked like adolescent girls."

"There are no male sirens. Their youthful beauty and high voices attract human or Aquapopulean males. If they mate they give birth exclusively to females." Suijin sat and leaned back on his elbows. "Sirens keep their young secluded until they reach maturity. The sisters gather like a pack to protect them. The young are alien-looking, somewhat deformed and out of proportion until they mature. Even I stay away from the mothers minding their offspring." He shrugged one shoulder. "It is the way of siren evolution," Suijin said matter-of-factly.

Harmony considered the life of a siren. Were they victims of evolution? One must lure, mate, and kill—or chose not to kill. "Why do they kill men? For that matter, why do they kill any of the Aquapopuleans? I've heard it's not just men they murder."

"It is true they have a thirst for blood—not much different from the tribes or humans, though the clans have remained the truest humanitarians."

When he looked at her his eyes turned polished and flat as mirrors. He lowered his voice. "If it's any consolation, the sirens fulfill a man's wildest desires before his final breath."

Maybe it was the husky bedroom voice he used, but an image of him among a group of sirens tending to his desires played in her head. Harmony thought if she were a cat her claws would be exposed, prepared to scratch out some eyes. She knew he took them as lovers; Luna had been eager to tell her so. They couldn't kill a god. Blinking like an owl, she desperately tried to replace the image with something else—anything else!

What has come over me? This is all because of that strange dream I had last night. It felt so real! Her mind replayed it. *If only I were free to take what he offered. No!*

That wasn't at all what she wanted...right?

Harmony turned her gaze toward the sea, indicating she'd lost interest in their conversation. She focused on steadying her breathing. The tranquil, rhythmic waves eased her pent-up nerves—until sirens swam into view.

Their dark heads bobbed in the waves as several made their way into the muddy river. Luna rose and stood knee-deep in the shallow water; muddy beads rolled down her boyish body. The others emerged to claim spots along the bank, not far from Suijin's feet, their bodies half in the water.

"Luna, you are just in time to do my back," Suijin called, sitting forward. Luna smiled sweetly at him and padded up the slight incline to kneel at his side.

"Get comfortable. I will care for you," she purred. She ran her wet fingers over the dried mud on his chest. At her suggestion, Suijin rolled over onto his stomach, resting his temple on his folded forearms.

Harmony, tense and alert, couldn't keep her eyes from darting to the couple. Luna reached for the saturated mud and worked the clay into his back. His long ebony lashes fluttered closed, and he sighed with pleasure while Luna blasted Harmony with a smug grin. It was the last straw

Harmony hopped to her feet and collected her hat from the bush. She retreated to an area a fair distance away from Suijin and his gathered harem and sat on the bank, her toes dangling in the water. She inhaled the salty air and took in the mountain view. It would almost be paradise if she were back in the human realm.

The mud had baked on and felt brittle and tight on her skin. She rolled the hat brim in her hands, wishing she could lie back, cover her face with it, and take a nap. But that wasn't happening with the sirens around. And though she considered wading into the water and washing off, her gaze drifted to the sirens gathered in the river's center. One siren stood in the waist-deep water, applying mud, while whispering and snickering to another. Both glanced in Harmony's direction.

Luna joined them to rinse her hands and arms. Harmony forced her gaze out to sea, not wanting to watch what looked like high school cheerleaders intimidating a book nerd—she being the book nerd. Their obvious snickers made Harmony's heartrate pick up a beat. When she glanced back, Luna strutted out of the water and approached Suijin, who sat on the ground beyond the river. Her heart raced faster when Luna seductively knelt and traced her finger over the mud swirls on Suijin's chest. They were well out of earshot, and she couldn't hear what Luna purred in his ear.

When she flicked her glance back to the siren pack, she saw one was advancing in her direction. She read the tallest siren's callous expression. The other two didn't dare to get as close to her as their taller friend. Harmony immediately felt heat coiling in her core, but she dragged in a breath to steady herself.

Mouth pulled into a sneer, the siren spoke. "You shouldn't be here. Luna is Suijin's companion. We," she swung her arm to include the rest of the sirens, "are his family."

Harmony had been there more than two months, and the sirens had become bolder. It was fine with her that Luna was Suijin's companion. Suijin had said the same, that the sirens were his family. Harmony didn't owe this siren any explanation, but she couldn't give it the satisfaction of knowing just how much she missed her own family. How desperately she missed Kodiak. This little act irritated Harmony beyond what she could bear.

How dare this siren speak to me like this!

"Family! Suijin took *my* family," Harmony barked. She sat forward, tossing her hat aside and warned, "You better get away from me." The malice in her voice surprised her. The heat slowly drifted down her arms, filling her veins with energy in its infant stage—she was still learning to control it—and it began to control her emotions. Silently she screamed at the siren in front of her: *Don't wake the beast! Don't unleash my wrath. You will be sorry!*

The siren seemed to consider her unvoiced warning. The tall one stepped back, shoulder to shoulder with her allies. The creature's eyes rounded with mock innocence and she cooed, "I watched the old woman drown. The sea serpent capsized the boat that she and her two friends were on. We held them underwater. I held *her* underwater. It was what Suijin asked of us. We would do anything for *our* family."

As the words registered in Harmony's mind, the vision played out in slow motion. The capsized boat had belonged to family friends, dear companions of Margret and Stan's, Harmony's grandparents. This siren had killed her grandmother. Suijin had allowed these creatures to cross and instructed they kill her friends and family!

The two sirens flanking the tall one snickered, smug looks on their faces. It would seem in their eyes they had proven to the human that they prevailed in these realms.

Harmony, poised for attack, growled through clenched teeth, "You bitch! You'll be sorry!"

The fear that crossed the sirens' faces gratified Harmony. As the mounting heat numbed her fingers, she lunged at the siren in the center. A disgruntled cry of rage tore from Harmony's throat, vibrating though the teeth she bared. One of her hands clamped on the siren's shoulder, burning into her bare flesh; the other landed on the face of the siren to her left. The third managed to dive away into the safety of the murky water. Harmony's focus was on the murderer she clutched. She didn't care that one got away. Or that the siren who grabbed her blistered red face had staggered back, wailing, sinking under the water to escape.

"You bitch—I'm going to kill you!" Harmony hissed, clutching the siren by the neck with her free hand. Somewhere in her mind a small voice pleaded that this was not who she was. She was not a killer. But she ignored her inner voice. She saw only red.

"You woke the beast!" She felt manic, and a delirious giggle bubbled. The siren's large eyes bulged, and her screams faded away.

"Harmony!" Suijin's deep, booming voice penetrated her brain. In her peripheral vision she saw he and Luna standing a few feet away on the bank.

Luna's demanding voice followed. "Release her, you monster!"

Harmony blinked. She watched the siren's eyes roll, near death. Peeling her palms from the burned flesh, Harmony let the siren sink. Her eyes circled the confines of the muddy river. The other sirens were swimming away, tears glistening in their horrified eyes.

Harmony's tunnel vision focused on the water god and the creature at his side. Mud dripped from her torso, loosened by the siren's splashes. Her make-shift bun hung loosely to one side. Several slack, wet locks freed during her mad dash into the waist-deep water clung to her neck and cheeks. She barely felt the silky water gliding past her thighs as she trudged purposefully toward the bank where the pair stood. Her eyes fixed on Luna. Every part of her body felt alive with energy. When she was like this, the foreign presence invading her body, she reveled in the power it gave her. In this high, she thirsted for blood.

When water splashed under her feet, Luna dove behind Suijin, who shielded her from Harmony's antagonistic approach.

"You're next, Luna," Harmony harassed, circling Suijin, who twisted to block her advancement on Luna.

"That's enough, Harmony. Stop!" Suijin's command was laced with anguish. "Please stop," he said more softly. He reached to clasp her arm.

Luna poked her head around his bicep and chirped, "She's a monster, Jin. Look what she did. She almost killed them!"

Harmony laughed bitterly. "You have no idea." She grinned deliriously.

The beast within her blackened her soul. In the fog of her memory, Finn had expressed this very warning. He'd cautioned that the abilities came from a powerful, dark place. What were they, she and Finn, part human and part Aquapopulean? Why had evolution allowed their creation?

"Luna," Suijin bellowed over his shoulder, never taking his eyes from Harmony. "Go home. Now!"

Luna skirted the man-god tower that stood between her and Harmony and scurried to the river. Harmony couldn't follow her despite her effort to shake Suijin off because he had captured her elbow in a vicelike grip.

He moved closer to her and lifted her chin with his knuckle. "Harmony, are you all right?"

The heat receded when Luna left her sight, and the energy, recoiled up her arms almost painfully. She took a shaky breath. The sensations from her core shuddered and left her momentarily panting. When she lifted her gaze to his, tears dribbled down her face, leaving streaks in the mud she'd patted there earlier. Suddenly feeling exhausted, she pushed the replaying images of what had just occurred into the recesses of her mind.

She realized her tears weren't remorse for what she'd done to those sirens but fear of what she was turning into.

"That siren told me...she drowned my..." Her words faltered as she glared into his ever-changing eyes, now a soft mossy green color. She knew burning the sirens upset him. She justified that he deserved to watch after what he'd taken from her. But when the god dropped to his knees before her and wrapped his arms around her torso, she was completely surprised.

"I'm so sorry. I beg your forgiveness." His dark head rested just below her chin and he murmured his words at her heart. "I realize now that I should have handled things differently. I don't like seeing you like this." Lifting his lips to press a kiss on the angle of her jaw, he said with emotion, "I am solely responsible, not the sirens. And I promise to make it up to you, Harmony."

Her tears stopped flowing the moment his confession began. To avoid touching him, her elbows were bent, her palms facing skyward. Her fingers twitched until she slowly lowered them to rest on his shoulders. While the last tears clung to her lashes, she searched his face.

She wanted to hate him.

But she didn't.

He'd admitted to his mistakes and begged her forgiveness. What did that say about him? Hadn't he disclosed his feelings for her? His active interest in her was mindboggling.

All this is temporary, she reassured herself. She said to the man-god who looked hopefully at her, "You know what I want."

She watched a shadow of pain cross his expression before he closed his eyes and ran the tip of his nose down her cleavage. When she squirmed, he reluctantly let her go.

He stood at his full height, towering over her. "Let's return to my palace." He held his hand out to her.

She took it.

12

The trip to the mud bath, yet another day of destruction branded in Harmony's mind, left her drained, mentally and physically. After their return to the island city, Suijin offered to carry her up the winding city road, but she refused. There was no way she was going to admit she struggled with every step up the steep slope. He offered assistance twice more but relented when she squared her shoulders and marched ahead.

As they passed through the kitchen, Harmony lifted a fruit bowl generously loaded with a variety of fruit into the crock of her arm without breaking her stride. Next she swiped a basket of bread. Suijin followed her up the steps and stopped at her doorway. Harmony crossed the threshold and turned to him.

"Jin, I'm going to eat, shower, and go to bed," she stated, devoid of emotion.

"I want to talk," he insisted, crossing the threshold.

Harmony set the food containers aside and clawed her fingers through her tangled hair. Her bun had unraveled against the bottom of the wooden boat during their return. Her hat had blown away and was forgotten. She sighed over the effort it would take to get her hair clean and smooth.

"I can't talk about what I did..." She squeezed her eyes shut.

"You must learn to control your emotions," he advised gently.

"What if I can't?" Her voice was strained.

"Harmony, you've only just learned about your gifts. It will take time to harness your powers. Give it time. I don't think you know how special you are or how talented. You've got so much potential. I feel you are destined for great things. While you are here I will help you in any way that I can." He cupped a large hand against her cheek. "I wonder if you are a gift to me."

Furrowing her brow, she shook her head slightly, not understanding his meaning.

"Perhaps the goddess felt sorry for what her husband did to me, locking me here in the dual earth realms. Maybe she has altered evolution to give you the power to resist me so I would notice you," he theorized.

"I'm not the only one with abilities."

"The tribal chieftain does not interest me," he said, looking amused at the idea.

Harmony figured Finn's power to harness the weather hadn't interfered with Suijin; therefore, he didn't consider the chief a threat or a nuisance. Suijin's comment rekindled her earlier thoughts about how she and Finn had come to exist.

"Can gods do that...alter evolution?" she whispered, astonished.

"The powerful ones can," he admitted.

Harmony caught his wrist, holding it still so he'd stop caressing her hair. "Jin..." She looked into his eyes, now a smoky sulfur-yellow. "Could you take away my ability so I can return to a normal life in the human realm?"

She saw his chest muscles flex, and his eyes shone brighter. "You don't want that. There is no going back to the mundane, *normal* life you think you had. It never really existed. You've always had your abilities—you *know* you are different and always have been."

Harmony released his wrist and shouldered herself away from him. She hated that he was right. Growing up as a girl raised by grandparents because her parents had drowned was tough. Though she loved her grandparents, being an only child added to the strange dynamic. Her classmates teased her because she was different, forcing her to turn her attention to reading. History, art, and architecture books became her sanctuary until Samantha Finch became her best friend. In the early years she'd learned to cope in solitude. Those old feelings of being an outcast now resurfaced. She ultimately wanted a full life and a family. She wanted to be around people who loved her.

"So I must embrace who I am?"

"Yes," he breathed, sounding relieved.

"But what if I don't like who I'm becoming? What if people don't accept me?" she challenged.

Suijin adjusted his stance and shifted his shoulders. "Harmony, your friends and family in this realm have already accepted you," he reminded her. "The Linker Calder has great faith in you. After all, he sent you back to the human realm confident you could help save their sacred island from further ruin. You made a sacrifice for those people. You personally overcame your fear when you crossed the realm to help your abducted human friend. And the Aquapopulean Diver, your husband, loves you for who you are."

She inhaled in shock at his mention of Kodiak. That comment didn't help his case for persuading her to want to remain here, but his next statement tugged at her heart.

"I love you for who you are, as well as what you are destined to become. I want you to open your mind. Don't be afraid. Look beyond the realms and you will find the answers you seek."

"Please, Jin…this is—"

She saw him struggle over his choice to hold her or let her be in peace. He sympathized. "Of course, you're tired. It's been an emotional day for us both." He nodded respectfully before moving to the door frame. Crossing into the hall, he murmured, "Sleep well, my love." Then he moved out of sight.

Harmony rushed forward to close the door for privacy. Leaning against the door, she vacantly stared at the food. Her stomach rumbled. But she remained immobile for several seconds. Overwhelmed, her back slid down the door until she sat on the cool stone floor. Drawing her knees to her chest, she wrapped her arms around them. Her shoulders sank, and she dropped her forehead and cried silently until the hot tears flushed out her anxieties.

Eventually she dragged herself to her feet. She ate just enough to satisfy her hunger. After a long shower, she crawled into bed. Her mind was too numb to recall the day's events again. Instead her eyes drifted shut until the sound of her own breathing was everything.

Shhk. Shhk. The sound of ice skates and her mother's voice mingled and filled her little ears. Harmony's breath was labored from her exertions. Her mother skated backward, holding her mitten-clad five-year-old's hands while she taught her how to ice skate. Suddenly a loud kachuck *and a cracking sound replaced the music of their laugher with screams.*

The ice separated and so did their hands. The section of ice Harmony stood on slanted, sliding her down the slippery slope into the icy water. Gravity pulled her under, where her absorbent clothes held her prisoner. She opened her eyes to the abyss below her. Through the blackness a face emerged. His handsome features showed no sign that he struggled to breathe. His cheeks didn't puff with air like hers. Who are you? Harmony wondered.

On some level of consciousness Harmony knew she was dreaming. But in this dream she was able to speak underwater, their thoughts communicating.

He answered in a clear and easy manner. "I'm the water god, here to kill you and your family."

Harmony sat up in bed, still half asleep, slashing at the sheets. Thinking she was still trapped underwater, she kicked her legs and clawed the air. She whimpered and moaned, "No...No!"

"Harmony! Harmony, I'm here." A deep voice penetrated her fog, and she blinked her eyes in the semi-dark room. It was the wee hours of the morning. Suijin sat on the edge of her bed and reached out to caress her damp hair.

As soon as she saw his face and his hand coming toward her, she smacked his arm away and rolled off the other side of the bed. She landed on all fours on the floor before she hopped up and staggered for several steps. Adrenaline coursed through her, and she was completely disoriented. At the sound of Suijin's voice she swatted at her hair that hung over her shoulder and looked suspiciously at the bed. When he rose up, she bolted. The white knee-length tunic she wore nearly glowed in the dark. He called to her as she passed over the threshold and ran barefoot down the hall.

The unlit hallways were closing in on her. She felt as claustrophobic as if she were underwater. She needed to get out—she needed to escape. One corridor replaced another, then another. She burst through several doors only to cry out when finding herself faced with another hallway. He was behind her, but how far? His voice echoed down the tunnel, making her head pound. She ran on, her limbs strangely heavy. Soon she felt a cramp start in her side. Another door came into view ahead. She heard his raised voice, booming loudly now.

"Stop! Harmony, stop!" He began to sprint up behind her, and his voice sounded closer, but she reached the door before he reached her.

The door led to a petite balcony, its banister no more than a ledge, and Harmony ran straight off the end of it.

The cold wind lifted her tunic, and her bare legs kicked to reach for a landing.

Mother, the ice! I'm falling into the water!

She was transported into her dream again.

Falling.

Falling.

She plummeted nearly three stories into the ocean.

The slapping force of the landing momentarily stunned her. She felt a million bubbles roll up her skin and the roots of her hair stretch up. Gravity and buoyancy began to come into play. Confused about what was happening, she opened her eyes and saw the water god swimming toward her, coming for her—the flashes of his scales caught her eye. A jolt of fear sparked her inner heat. At lightning speed, the bolt of energy shot down her arms. As Suijin grabbed her waist with both hands and thrust her up toward the surface, her hand flattened against his chest. She felt his body jolt, but he didn't let go. Her lungs started to burn after her exceptionally deep plunge. Although she was quickly running out of oxygen she was too disoriented to realize it or the fact that Suijin was trying to save her from drowning. She fought on, knowing her fingers were burning his flesh. Quickly the searing fizzled. It was too late. She'd swallowed too much seawater. Her body went limp.

Suijin broke the surface holding Harmony in his arms. A swell rapidly pushed the couple to the shore. He laid her on a flat rock. She was motionless only a moment before she convulsed and coughed violently. Water spewed from her mouth before she rolled to her stomach, coughing again. After she caught her breath, she rested her forehead on the back of her hand. Turning her head slightly, she saw the tip of the orange sun just rising on the horizon. All was silent except the surf, and she listened, allowing her pulse to slowdown.

Fully awake, her brain started to question what she was doing outside, soaking wet, lying on a slab of rock. *I was dreaming that awful dream again. And Suijin chased me into the sea. No...that's not what happened. I was running from him and he was trying to wake me—to warn me to stop. I fell...he jumped in to save me. And I hurt him!* She pushed up on her elbow to look for him. He was sprawled out a few feet away, leaning back on his elbows, watching her.

"Jin!" She crawled to him and stared in horror at the charred marks across his chest. The bubbled skin was red. "I'm so sorry. I didn't know...I was dreaming..." She knelt beside him, her hair in sodden waves at her cheeks. Her hand paused at his shoulder as she realized that he'd returned to his god-like state. Scales gleamed down his arms and legs. *That's why I could hurt him.*

"I'm okay. I'll heal. Just like the last time," he said tightly, clearly in pain. He indicated the scars and grinned at her, his eyes as gold-orange as the newly rising sun.

"Right," she stammered. The scars from the last time she'd burned him remained. Harmony had thought he was trying to drown her that day. She had been wrong about him—just like the Aquapopuleans. She continued to hold her hands helplessly in the air. "What can I do? I'm afraid to touch you."

"You don't need to do anything, but remember—you can control it." He stretched his palm out to allow her to touch him. He added, "Are you all right?"

She knew his outstretched hand was meant for her to test her ability, but she didn't trust herself. The pain seemed to turn his irises dark orange now. For a moment, Kodiak's cooper eyes flashed in her mind, but she couldn't think of Kodiak now. She had to help Suijin inside, possibly find Luna to help him. Tentatively, she touched the tip of her middle finger to his palm. Nothing happened. She relaxed her hand against his. Her other hand hesitantly skimmed his shoulder, and when she detected no heat, she let her hand slip over his shoulder and down his bare back. She helped him sit up, rising on her knees to do so.

Her torso was pressed against the length of his arm. Suijin's other hand cupped her chin, holding her still while he looked her over. "You appear to be unharmed." He breathed a sigh of relief.

She gave a teensy nod. "I'm fine." She rolled her eyes and grumbled, "It was stupid of me to run...I was so careless falling off that ledge! Honestly, I didn't realize what I was doing." His hand still cupped her cheek, so she lifted only her eyes to see how far up the balcony hung. "I could have hit those rocks." She dropped her gaze back to his. She watched a pulse of red swirl in his irises before he closed his eyes and kissed her forehead.

"I could not bear it if you had."

"Jin!" she said with anguish. "How can you want me? Even if I wanted to stay...it couldn't work between us. I have too many nightmares from my past—nightmares you gave me!"

"I can erase your past."

"What? No! Never!" When she grabbed his wrist it sizzled at her touch. She released it immediately. Lifting her hand from his back, she sat back on her heels. "Please, never take away my memories. Promise me!"

He nodded and rotated his wrist. They both glanced at the insignificant burn mark she'd left there. She noticed the wounds on his chest begin to scab over.

"I can't always control it, though I just did for a minute."

"You will," he said confidently. "And I promise I won't take away your memories, unless you change your mind. Then I'd fill your head with nothing but pleasant thoughts of me." He gave her a smirk.

Harmony sniffed and laughed despite herself. "You're hopeless." She stood and gathered the length of the tunic around her knees. The saturated fabric hanging from her torso felt like it weighed fifty pounds. She attempted to wring it out, but the heavy, wet fabric clung to her. She was desperate to get inside and change.

"Can you get up?" she asked. Suijin had remained seated on the rock, watching her. With a deep inhale, he rose to his feet. Harmony was grateful she wouldn't have to summon Luna for help.

Later, Suijin left her in her room with instructions to change and meet him in his chamber for breakfast. She stripped off her tunic and laid it by the window to dry in the sunshine. The sun was above the horizon line now, and she stared at it while she toweled her hair. She remembered their conversation; she'd asked him how he could want her. He was a god, while she was a mere mixed-race earthling. And she wasn't even one-of-a-kind—Finn was also mixed race. Finn was half human and half Aquapopulean. She was maybe a quarter Aquapopulean? Perhaps Suijin was right that it was her ability that attracted him. After all, some guys want what they can't have. It was extreme that she could fight him off with her ability, and she'd just made him suffer again, yet in all his godly glory he took it.

Her fingertips brushed her forehead where he'd kissed her. His irises had briefly swirled red. *What did that mean?* She'd learned the changing colors were a window into his emotions, though she couldn't know them all.

He'd said he couldn't bear it if she'd hit the rocks. Apparently he couldn't bring back the dead.

13

The Human Realm

Kodiak hung the kitchen phone up. Mike Coombs had called and graciously offered him another job. Mike said there were numerous wrecks off the Florida coast—enough work to keep them busy for years. Nearly four months had passed since he'd come home from the Great Lakes expedition. He'd passed on the two jobs Mike had previously offered, not wanting to risk missing Harmony coming home.

But after all this time Harmony still had not returned.

Strangely, her best friend, Samantha Finch, had gone missing around the same time Harmony left. Kodiak began to wonder if the girls were together. Would Harmony allow Samantha to take such a treacherous journey through the portal? Of course, only Kodiak knew about the other realm, and he couldn't tell anyone. So at first he'd mentioned to Mr. Finch that the girls had talked about spending time together and taking a vacation, hoping to squelch the man's fears. At that time he'd believed his wife would return within a week or maybe two.

After two weeks Mr. Finch got the police involved. They questioned Kodiak, but he had an alibi. He'd flown in five days after they'd gone missing. As the weeks went on and no word came from the girls, Kodiak tried to avoid Mr. Finch.

Damn it Harmony, I can't wait any longer! Maybe it was time for him to move on too.

Though Kodiak enjoyed diving the wreckage in the human realm, it was not worth being here without his wife. He strode down the hallway into the den and paused in the middle of the room, rubbing the back of his neck and contemplating taking out the herbs. With a frustrated growl he skirted the desk and pulled open the bottom draw. He lifted the tin and slammed it on the desk. There were no warning labels on the container, but Kodiak knew there were serious risks. He wasn't a Linker, made for realm crossings, yet he'd gone through with Harmony relatively unscathed. He had been deathly ill and lost his Diver's ability to remain underwater for long periods, but he'd made it through in one piece. It was worth it to be with the woman he loved. That's why he'd take the risk of crossing again to find her.

He popped the lid and dumped the contents on a silver letter tray. Then he fished around in the desk drawers for matches. He paused a moment, the matches clutched in his sweaty palm, considering whether he should take anything or do anything…

No. I just need to do this. Go find Harmony. Nothing else matters. He struck the match and dropped the tiny flame on the dried herbs.

I'm coming to you, my love.

The smell reached him first, and then his lungs tightened as if he'd dived too deep. The herbs smoldered and smoked, discharging poison at a lethal rate. The sickness felt like the bends, and he hit the floor hard when he fell. His fingernails dug into the carpet as he violently coughed. He welcomed the blackness…

Blackness surrounded him. Kodiak sucked in air and realized he wasn't underwater. Had he already crossed and someone pulled him on land? There was softness under his palm—stiff but soft, like wool. Wool carpet. He snapped his eyes open to stare at the pattern on the wool carpet in the den. He shot upright, only making it to his elbows because his head was swimming. With one eye closed and the other squinting, he looked, bleary-eyed, around the room. He was still in Stanley Parker's den. The herbs had not worked. They hadn't sent him back to the Aquapopulean realm. He remained stuck in the human realm without Harmony Parker.

The Aquapopulean Realm

As the end of the human calendar year approached, Suijin knew he had tried everything he could think of to make Harmony comfortable here. Still she resisted opening up to him, despite those few rare times when she'd let her guard down, like when curiosity engaged her in lengthy conversations or when he heard her laughter. Her kisses had branded his heart, and he lived just to kiss her again.

He had been tolerant of her abuse to his sirens that day on the muddy banks. Knowing the sirens were vicious, he reckoned they would learn the hard way to respect Harmony. After that day, the sirens had shied away from him, bickering among themselves because he'd changed. Had he? Most nights he was restless and couldn't sleep. Though gods didn't sleep like humans and animals, they did rest in a state of deep meditation.

Tonight he'd gone for a swim. The portal lay just beneath him as Suijin floated on his back and gazed at the moon glowing over the rippling water. He was in the human realm. He'd just been inside Harmony Parker's house, looking at the evidence of her previous life, wanting a fuller understanding of her. He'd sensed the place was empty before he'd entered.

After wandering through the rooms he'd entered the study, where he found an envelope addressed to Harmony. He sank into the leather chair and read it.

Harmony,

I returned from the *SS Edmund Fitzgerald* expedition to find you gone. I regret taking so long to return from Lake Michigan. Your note states that you are with your family—I understand how hard it is for you to travel so far! Although I don't understand why you left, I'm even more confused about why you have not come back to me. I hope you are well and safe. I've been offered another expedition in Florida and have decided to take the job. Without you, this is all that I have. After these long months I can only assume that you have moved on. I'm sorry everything has been so complicated. If you find this note...know that I love you and hope we see each other again.

Your devoted husband,
Kodiak

Suijin returned to the water with the letter in his hand. He set it to drift and watched it sink. It seemed the minor complication regarding Harmony's husband had rectified itself.

The sun was rising in the Aquapopulean realm when Suijin emerged from the ocean. Suijin noted the cooler breeze that gusted through the staggered and abandoned buildings on the road to the palace. He'd gone to great trouble to alter the currents to bring warmer water and air temperatures and wondered if Harmony noticed the change. Carried on the wind was the sound of a woman crying, and he quickened his pace. Distressed, he followed the sound through several adjoining structures. Eventually, he saw Harmony sitting in the dry grass in an old courtyard, plucking the needles from a tiny pine tree.

"Harmony! What are you doing out here? Why are you crying?" Suijin rushed to her side and knelt beside her.

"I've keep track of the days I've been here," she said accusingly. "And today...well, today is Christmas." This announcement brought a stifled cry. She held her fist to her lips, and her shoulders pumped with grief.

"Christmas? The human Christian holiday?" Suijin didn't see the connection. He couldn't understand what had upset her. "Harmony, I am the only god of these realms. That is silly paganism."

She sent an angry look his way and gushed, "Not for me or my family. Christmas is always special. I'm supposed to be sharing it with my husband, not spending it here in this freezing forsaken place."

Lines appeared above Suijin's thick brows. *Harrumph. She is cold?* Apparently his strenuous efforts to alternate the currents weren't appreciated. Annoyed, he *tsk*ed. "Your husband is long gone. You needn't concern yourself about him any longer."

"What are you talking about?"

"You married an underwater treasure hunter. Surely that is the Diver's first love."

"You're wrong! He's probably waiting for me right now—desperately waiting for me to return. I told him I would come back."

"I doubt that."

"What do you know about it? He loves me. Just take me home. You'll see."

"If I take you to your house and he is not there...if fate proves otherwise, would you return with me and dedicate yourself to getting to know me better?"

Suijin watched her gaze rest once again on the small pine tree. Her fingertips brushed its needles; she seemed to consider his words. Finally she turned bright eyes toward him. "Take me home right now. If Kodiak isn't there I will come back with you and stay a little while longer. But I will not stay your prisoner forever."

Suijin was quick to agree.

"But," she insisted, "if he's there, you have to leave me there and promise to never bother me or my family again.

"I will agree if we kiss on it."

Harmony rolled her eyes but nodded. She stood and wiped away a sniffle. In one swift movement Suijin stood and reached for her. He slipped his arms around her waist and pulled her close.

"A real kiss," he clarified.

He knew she couldn't say no. And he knew he would win their wager. He smiled with confidence and dropped his mouth to hers. Her lips were stiff and cold—at first. They softened as he stroked them with his own firm and warm lips. One of his large hands traveled up her back and cupped the nape of her upturned head. The other hand imprisoned the small of her back. With her secured, he deepened his kiss.

He felt her fist strike at his bicep, indicating she wanted him to release her. Apparently she was refusing to touch him. But he didn't want to stop yet. Elated that she would be open to him in the days to come, he continued his exploration. His tongue glided along the seam of her lips and pushed through them to sweep the cavity of her sweet mouth. Her squirming only heightened his arousal. She immediately ceased when he groaned at the effect of her movements. He was in— invading. His tongue ran along her teeth and poked the inner velvet of her cheek. He felt her grip his shoulders. He dueled with her tongue until her fingernails dug into his flesh. He pulled back before capturing her lips again. He slowly opened his eyes to gaze upon her lovely face. She opened her eyes too. What he saw surprised him.

***

Harmony imagined being reunited with her husband—and imagined this was her good-bye to Suijin. Despite their turbulent time together, she knew he loved her. And though she couldn't label her feelings for him as either attraction or affection, she knew she no longer feared or hated him. For a fleeting moment when she looked into his magnificent turquoise eyes after their passionate kiss, she wondered what it would be like to truly love him. But she couldn't allow that thought to linger, and she pulled away from his embrace.

"I'm ready to leave," she announced a bit breathlessly. She didn't want to give him time to change his mind.

Suijin nodded, a faint smile on his lips. He reached for her hand and led her back down to the shore.

"Wait. Where is the boat?" Her query was laced with apprehension.

"You cannot cross the realm in a boat. Hold onto me and take a deep breath. We will be there in a few moments. Can you do that? Can you trust me?" He seemed to probe beyond her eyes into her soul.

She swallowed her panic, because she couldn't let fear ruin her opportunity. And she did trust him. She trusted that he wouldn't hurt her or allow anything to happen to her. Licking her lip, she nodded.

The pair waded in, and Harmony faced him to place her arms around his neck. She clung to him for dear life, squeezing her eyes tight. After a deep breath she felt their immersion, and then quickly she was lifted out of the water. As Suijin carried her to the back porch of her house, she opened her eyes to see they were crossing snow-covered grass in the dark. She glanced at the house next door and saw the Christmas tree illuminating their window. With one glance over Suijin's broad shoulder, she confirmed it was predawn from the way the sun's rays were lightening the sky.

He set her down once they were inside the porch. Shivering from the cold, she moved to the vase where the hidden key was stored. Her hands shook with excitement and anticipation, and she struggled with the door. Inside, she turned to Suijin. "Maybe you should wait outside. If Kodi sees you..."

Suijin hung back and crossed his arms, giving her a head start. She smiled gratefully and rushed away. She dashed through the kitchen and down the hallway to the living room. She assumed he was asleep at this early hour and jogged up the stairs. When she reached the threshold of their bedroom she was near tears, her anticipation so great.

Harmony stood paralyzed in the doorway for a moment. The made bed was empty. She immediately swiveled and padded down the hallway to her grandparent's old bedroom leaving wet footprints.

Maybe he is sleeping in here? No. Empty.

"Kodi!" she called to the empty house. "Kodi!" she hollered again.

No! This can't be possible. This can't be happening! Did he leave me? She moved to their bedroom closet, where she'd made room for Kodi to keep his new clothes. She swung the door open and stared dumbfounded at the naked hangers. *His clothes are gone! He's gone!*

She dove face first onto her bed, releasing a hoarse and tormented cry into the quilt. Each breath against the fabric evoked memories, and she continued to sob for several minutes. She remembered her previous doubts about their unusual relationship and wondered if things would have worked out if she'd stayed and not gone off to rescue Samantha.

When her tears subsided, she was curled in a ball on top of her wrinkled quilt. Her eyes felt puffy as she tried to focus on the sunrise beyond her bedroom window, framed in pink lace curtains. She listened to Suijin's heavy steady footsteps on the staircase and blinked her burning eyes when he called her name from the doorway.

With a shaky breath she rose on her elbows and then swiveled around to sit at the edge of the bed. Unceremoniously, she rubbed her eyes and then reached for a tissue on her nightstand. She blew her nose loudly and tossed the tissue onto the floor. *Who cares about this place? I may never return. I might be destined to live among my other family in the Aquapopulean realm.* She glanced around at her childhood home. The home her grandparents raised her in. But they were gone. Even her best friend from next door, Samantha, would never again return to this house.

"He's gone." Her voice was void of emotion.

"Hmm, he is far from these waters," he murmured.

She blinked her puffy eyes and sniffed. "What do you mean? How do you know that?"

"I know where the underwater creatures are—except in the North and South Pole, where the ice acts like a wall and blocks my powers. I sense he is here in this realm, but the vibe is faint, which means he's likely thousands of miles from here."

"Oh. Then you knew he wasn't here?"

He shrugged.

He'd tricked her and let her get her hopes up. She felt stupid but admitted to herself that she'd had to see for herself that Kodi was truly gone.

Harmony reached for another tissue and dabbed at her nose. It was astounding that Suijin could sense underwater beings. After thinking about it, she asked for clarification. "You can't sense anything through the ice?"

"Nor can I break it with my abilities."

"You didn't break the ice my mother and I fell through? Yet you knew we fell into the water." Harmony read the remorse in his eyes and understood he took no pleasure in seeing her in pain.

"I did not touch it. Some things are up to fate, but I was always watchful. Once you both were in the water I was there in an instant."

She knew the rest. She nodded bleakly. Evolution, the gods, fate…whatever had caused her life to plunge out of whack seemed inevitable. Where would she ultimately end up? What would become of her and those she loved? With new resolve, she rose from the bed and faced him. She said simply, "Let's go."

The man-god standing before her in her home was larger than life. A god from the universe in her home! He tenderly pressed his palm to her cheek, chasing away remnant tears with his thumb. "I'm sorry, my love."

The compassion in his voice allowed her to lean against his palm for comfort. Kodiak was gone. Suijin was here for her. "Take me back, Jin. I don't want to be here right now."

When they reached the study door she paused and placed her fingertips on the knob. On impulse she opened it and scanned the room. Nothing was amiss. Just as quickly she pulled the door closed. She left the house and walked to the water, Suijin quiet at her side. When she was last in that room she'd burned the herbs and crossed the realms to find Samantha. No sign of the herbs remained on the desk. She assumed Kodiak must have stashed them away before he packed a bag and left.

Why didn't he use them? He could have tried to find me. Am I not worth the risk? Did he not understand I couldn't come back? That I was kept from him? Why did he give up on us?

Preparing for their underwater journey, she wrapped her arms around the man who loved and accepted her. She swallowed her grief and fear and hugged him, this time with affection.

14

In the weeks that followed, Harmony was willing to be more open with Suijin. They enjoyed long walks and sunset dinners, and she allowed him to steal an occasional kiss goodnight. She tried with all her will to block Kodiak from her mind, but at night when her longing for him broke the barriers she often cried herself to sleep. She was desperate to be out of this funk—to move on and mend her broken heart.

Late January in New England it was typically thirty degrees. The place Suijin took her to one day was closer to seventy degrees, though the ocean temperature was well below that. He'd shuttled them south to a rocky coast with hot springs. After a long soak in the hot springs, Harmony stretched in the afternoon sun. She'd had a rather nice day with Suijin and was feeling sleepy and content. She watched him from under her lashes. He rose out of the pool, flexing his muscles and slowly slicking his black hair back from his angular face. He glanced her way, and she averted her eyes. When he stretched out beside her she imaged two honeymooners on vacation. She screwed her eyes shut.

Stop thinking things like that!

"There is so much I can give you."

The nearness of his baritone voice prompted her to roll her head and look at him.

"I'd like to return to my clan family. I've been here far too long," she reminded him.

"Trust me, Harmony. My gifts will change your life," he hinted mysteriously. "I'll be right back." He hopped up, jogged to the beach, and dove into the waves.

She opened her mouth to call out, "I like my life," but in truth she was unsure where her life was headed. She wondered how Kodiak's expedition had gone, if he'd returned to her home looking for her, or if he'd just moved on to something else more interesting without giving her any thought. It didn't matter now. She believed returning to the human realm after his disappearance might prove to be too painful. She was still licking her wounds after rejection and abandonment. Maybe she shouldn't have been so surprised to find Kodi gone. After all, she'd been out of reach for months.

Her eyes scanned the sea, looking for a sign of Suijin. She wouldn't be his prisoner forever—no matter how pleasant he often made her days. Her recent heartbreak had left her open to other possibilities. She disliked that she spent time wondering what it would be like to spend eternity with a god. The heart wants what the heart wants—could the heart have two desires?

Suijin climbed out of the waves, his dark hair shiny against his bronze skin. Harmony's eyes widened when she noticed his scales—he'd changed into his godly form.

Why?

The instant he dropped beside her, sending droplets across her salty skin, she asked, "Why did you change? I still can't control my abilities, Jin. I don't want to accidentally hurt you."

"Hush, my love. I want to give you a gift. Just relax," he soothed.

Looking at Suijin, his eyes as blue as the sky, forced her to see how much he cared for her. He often brought her gifts, but she sensed this one was something magical. Suddenly she felt nervous and exposed in her bikini with him intimately at her side. He rarely changed to his god-like form around her. What could he gift her here in the middle of nowhere?

She rose on her elbows, but he placed his hand across her abdomen, stopping further movements. She tried not to squirm at his imitate touch and stared him down. He tried to hide his grin. A mask of calm washed over his face and his eyes closed. She froze, trying to control her fear, not wanting to inadvertently hurt him.

His breathing became steady. She felt the weight of his heavy hand on her skin. Her eyes roamed his handsome face. His eyes slowly opened, and she watched colors swirl in his irises. A jolt of desire shot through her. She'd learned to covet his unusual trait and was always captivated by it.

"Do you feel it?" He slowly moved his palm in a circular motion.

Her eyes blinked several times. She felt heat penetrating deep into her body where his hand moved.

"What are you doing?"

She was concerned he had a similar ability to hers. Would she somehow get burned? She shook her head, wanting him to stop.

"Like I said, I'm giving you a gift. Relax. It won't hurt," he said, and he slid his strong hand up her ribcage.

The heat intensified, but there was something more. Her lungs began to tighten as his fingers spanned her breasts. She could not speak, and she dropped her head back, attempting to suck in as much air as she could. An invisible energy—an unbending, magnetic energy—held her body against his hand. She arched her back, scarcely able to take a shallow breath. What he was doing didn't hurt exactly, but it frightened her immeasurably. She was suspended for several minutes in a tense posture. Perhaps her ability could break the spell, but she dared not summon it.

When he released his paralyzing hold on her, her limbs were weak. He supported her head and gently guided it to the ground. She deeply inhaled glorious air and exhaled with relief when he removed his hands from her.

"What did you do to me?" She felt strange and touched her ribs and chest where his hand had been. She lifted her head and saw only her unmarred skin. Her questioning gaze returned to his face. Something was off.

"What the hell did you do to me, Jin?" She sat up in a huff.

"Come into the sea and I'll show you." He stood and offered her his hand.

"No! Not until you tell me," she insisted. She didn't want to play games with a god. *Who knows what he is capable of?*

Suijin seemed to give up his hope to surprise her. He confessed, "You don't have to be afraid of the ocean's depths. I gifted you with the lung capacity of the Aquapopuleans. You are now able to stay underwater as long as their best Diver can."

At his mention of Divers, her heart constricted. Kodiak was a Diver. Her husband had lost this very ability when he'd crossed into her realm. How ironic how she possessed it now!

"Well? Are you willing to give it a try?" he asked, holding his hand out to her.

Stunned, she could only nod. His words gave her hope; overcoming her fear would be monumental. The irrational fear of deep water held her back, and she wanted desperately to be free of it. Accepting his hand, she stood and allowed him to lead her to the water's edge.

Can this be true? Could this work?

She hesitated, her belly cramping with anxiety.

"Harmony, I only want to do right by you. I want to make amends for what I did to your family. Now that I know you and how much they meant to you... I cannot bring them back, but I can take away some of your apprehension. I don't want you to blame me for your fears any longer. You don't have to be afraid anymore. Just take a deep breath," he urged. "I'll be right there with you the entire time. I promise."

Harmony's pattern of blaming him for everything began to slip. This world was complicated, and she couldn't fathom what existed beyond these realms. Though he was a god cast here from somewhere in the universe, he was acting more human and trying to make amends. He was making up for it in an immense way by giving her an ability she'd never thought possible.

She tentatively said, "All right, I'd like to try. But Jin…" She drew back on his hand to halt his progress. "The water…it's just that…the water is so cold." She smiled sheepishly, thinking her human limitations would always be a weakness.

Suijin seemed to consider this issue. "I will take you to warmer waters. I will move us instantly to the equator. Remember, like before? Just hold on to me tightly." He lifted her in his arms.

Though they'd used this mode of travel a few times, she couldn't help saying, "You know I prefer to travel by boat."

"Not for long." He flashed his white teeth.

She swallowed hard. She couldn't help looking to see what color his irises were at this moment. They were tranquil blue, but she was looking for something more… Could she trust him? He smiled broadly and secured her bikini-clad body in his arms. She clasped her hands behind his neck and tightened them when he entered the water.

"Are you ready?" he asked, their faces inches from each other.

"Yes. I trust you, Jin." Her chest rose and fell at a rapid rate. She saw the expression change on his handsome face, but when his irises swirled to black her stomach flip-flopped.

At the sting of freezing water, she quickly gulped in a huge breath before she was submerged. Her entire body tingled from the tiny bubbles that rippled over her body as Suijin rocketed them into clear and calm warmer water. She screwed her eyes closed, hugging Suijin like a drifter on a raft. Then she felt him slow, and the pressure decreased. They broke the surface, and a gentle breeze caressed her face. She opened her eyes and inhaled oxygen.

"We are here. Are you feeling okay?" he asked. He released her legs and moved his hands to rest on her hips underwater.

He didn't need to tread water; she clung to him as though he were standing on dry ground. Harmony slipped her arms from his shoulders and floated back so their bodies no longer touched.

"Yeah, that was…exhilarating." Harmony was ready now to erase her anxiety. "I want to go under."

"Okay. Take in a long slow breath and hold it. Relax. I won't leave your side."

She felt like a kid on a thrill ride from the excitement, but she did as he said and took in a long, slow breath. They slipped under the salty sea.

The warm water caressed her skin as she dove down. Though the salt stung her eyes at first, soon she couldn't get enough of the tranquil color—similar to the color of his irises earlier. She glanced at him; his now-onyx gaze never left her, and she wondered at this beautiful man-fish who swam next to her. Sunlight filtered through and reflected off his shimmering scales.

The light was faded at this depth, and she paused to float, using her hands to propel her in a circle. A large fish moved silently and smaller fish bounced along beside it. Schools of brightly colored triangle fish moved at a steady pace until they turned sharply to dart in another direction. Several minutes passed. Harmony marveled at this gift. She turned full circle, and Suijin pointed to something. As a sea serpent floated like a kite on the wind toward them, Harmony vibrated with fear. She swam closer to Suijin, her eyes wild. She jabbed a finger at the surface.

Suijin held his hand up to quiet her fears as the giant dragon-like head bobbed nearer. Harmony knew she couldn't scream. Suijin turned to face the approaching beast while Harmony rapidly kicked her feet to stay behind him. She placed her hands on his shoulders.

Suddenly she felt the heat build in her hands—and apparently so did Suijin. He clasped her hands abruptly and shook his head at her. Afraid that she'd accidentally burn him, she pulled her hands away. The sea serpent was closer now, and Suijin stretched his hand toward it. As it passed by, it dipped its head, as if bowing with respect to the god. Harmony watched Suijin's hand run along the serpent's scaled neck.

The sea creature sailed by, its front half disappearing into the darker water, but then it turned and snaked its way back. When it thrust its horned head in Harmony's direction, energy blew from her palms, like a flame igniting. The serpent's head reared back, as if punched by an underwater boxing glove. Its body looped before it swam away. Harmony's relief was temporary. When she looked at Suijin, his angry expression frightened her. He simply pointed up and swam in that direction.

The sky looked amazing from beneath the clear sea as she approached the surface. Smoothly breaking the surface, she inhaled fresh air. She'd done it! She stayed underwater for about ten minutes, she guessed. Except when that sea serpent had come along, her fear had seemed under control. She had to thank Suijin for this gift. It was truly life altering. Something in her had changed.

However, she found she was reluctant to speak first.

"Harmony, you mustn't hurt my creatures. I was with you. No harm will ever come to you when I'm with you," he scolded.

"I know. I'm sorry. That thing scared me. I couldn't help it," she said to justify her automatic response. She traced the scales on his shoulder to distract him from his anger.

He easily forgave her.

"You are getting better at monitoring your ability. At least with me." He grinned. "I wasn't sure what kind of a jolt I would receive when I touched you to expand your lung capacity."

"You were lucky! I was scared to death about what you were doing to me."

They smiled at each other, silent with their thoughts.

After a moment, Harmony proposed, "I'd like to see more—but no serpents or sirens…or sharks either."

"Nothing scary, I promise," he vowed. "Your playground awaits you."

They frolicked for hours. Finally she wrapped her arms around him, and he jetted them like a high-speed submarine back to his island. She staggered out from the waves, her limbs heavy. The early evening air was cooling down, so she found a sunny spot to dry off. The soft warm sand was inviting. She'd never felt so exhilarated and exhausted at the same time.

The setting sun was veiled by wispy clouds that defused the glare. Her heavy-lidded eyes roved over Suijin as he approached.

If only my life wasn't so complicated…

She hushed her thoughts. She'd come to know him as he'd wanted, but what did that prove? So she'd come to care for him? What of it? If he were just a man she'd met in a coffee shop, that would be entirely different, wouldn't it? Although he'd given her this exceptional gift and shown her nothing but kindness, he was responsible for killing her family. Still, he'd shown remorse and apologized.

She wondered if a god was truly capable of love. Yes. The answer was yes, because she felt love in the way he caressed her and the way he looked at her. It seemed he didn't give out gifts to just anyone. In all his years in these realms he'd granted Sirena and Luna the ability to walk on land and to extend their lives. He'd offered to extend *her* life eternally. She thought their story read like a tale from Greek mythology.

After the long day of entertaining, Suijin, smiling and looking content, dropped to the sand beside her. She was leaning back on her elbows, and he blocked the sun with his broad shoulders.

"Can you make it to the palace or do I have to carry you?" his deep voice teased.

She swatted at his arm good-naturedly. "I swam for hours, Jin. My muscles feel like jelly."

"Hmm. I can help you with that."

"Yeah? You can take away the soreness?" she asked. She dropped her head back onto a pillow of sand. The thought crossed her mind that it would take her forever to get the sand out of her hair, but she was blissfully relaxed.

"I can." He rolled to face her and dropped his hand on her arm. Under the pressure of his thumb on her bicep, she closed her eyes and sighed.

Harmony allowed herself to relax deeper by slowing her breathing. The weight of his hand on her skin was pleasant as it moved across her collarbone. When it slid between her breasts, his fingers brushing the edges of her bikini top, her eyes popped open.

"What are you doing?" she asked accusingly, but her voice was amused.

He slid his hand to a stop and rested it on her stomach. "I can make you forget about your soreness."

She pressed her lips together so she wouldn't smile. She'd thought he had some godly power, that he'd just zap her and she would stop feeling sore. Obviously he had other ideas.

"Oh, I don't think massaging me or any other activity is going—"

He laughed deeply and suddenly tickled her ribs, catching her off guard. She squealed. His size and sheer strength overmatched her, but she zapped him with her energy until he rolled on his back and released her. She rolled with him, landing on his lap. With her hands by his ears, careful not to touch him, she waited for the tingling friction to dissipate. Then a jolt of vitality surged through her, taking her breath away. She stared down at Suijin as she wrapped her mind around this foreign feeling. She was reluctant to admit what it was. The potent energy pulsing down her arms and the powerful god pinned between her thighs, helpless against her energy and will, gave her the ultimate high. She felt divinely dominant—and wicked—and she liked it.

"What's happening to me?" she whispered.

He didn't move a muscle. His expression softened before he grinned at her. "You are becoming stronger—as I knew you would. You are no ordinary human, Harmony. You are extraordinary."

"You've altered me."

"I didn't alter you… I enhanced you."

When the heat evaporated from her hands, she sat back, dropping them on her thighs. Her gaze shifted to his long black hair, half buried in the sand. She noticed the strand of blond hair woven in it. She was changing, she knew, but into what she couldn't guess. This wasn't the first time she'd felt a high like this. In fact, it almost always followed when she used her ability, though she buried it with guilt. It was as if dark magic were sucking her in, but she didn't like tricks. What would Calder say...or Kodiak? Would they understand what she was going through? How could she go back to her old life after her transformation?

Her little town of New Castle seemed so far away...the Wentworth cause meaningless while she remained tucked away in this realm with a god who loved her. She crossed her arms against her chest and leaned forward to lay on top of him. She rested her cheek against the strong beat of his heart. Her legs still straddled him. She nestled against him, if only for a little while, needing his comfort. His arms protectively closed over her. She felt his bunched muscles under her cheek when he lifted his head to place a kiss against her hair. Her eyelids felt heavy, and they closed, blotting out her thoughts. Her breathing became even.

"Harmony?" Suijin softly called her name.

"Mmm." Her eyes fluttered open. She wondered if she'd fallen asleep. Indeed she had, for it was quite dark now.

"You're getting cold. Let's go inside." He was rubbing his hands over her goose-fleshed skin.

"Oh. I guess I must have drifted off," she said. She pushed herself up to a sitting position. She quickly realized she still intimately straddled his hips, and she swung her leg off him to kneel in the sand. She winced when her particularly sore thigh muscles protested.

They both stood up to brush sand from their bodies and then they headed toward the town. Harmony's siesta had revived her a bit, and she realized she hadn't thanked Suijin for giving her the lung capacity of the Aquapopulean clans.

"Jin, today...you gave me an incredible gift. No longer being afraid of deep water has lifted a weight off my shoulders. So thank you."

He grinned at her, but his brow knit pensively. "You would not have had the fear in the first place if not for me—after what I did to your mother. I wanted to make it right. I've given you this gift so you can find peace and allow the water to calm you instead of upset you. I hope I've made that loss up to you in some small way," he said sincerely.

"The truth is I don't remember my parents at all. My grandparents raised me, and I never wished it to be any different. They were amazing together—true soulmates. After my grandfather died, my grandmother was never the same. In the three years without him, she aged."

"Harmony—"

"It's okay. It's done now. After you took my grandfather, it was best that you took her too. If what you say is true and their souls have reunited, then it was for the best." She didn't voice the sinister thought that she wouldn't want her grandparents to see that she was becoming a monster.

"Hold on. I want to tell you about your grandfather."

She waited, wondering what he had to say.

"The night his car went off the bridge, he suffered extensive internal damage. Technically, he wouldn't have survived the ambulance ride. His soul released once he drowned," he said.

"You eased his suffering?" She guessed his meaning.

"Yes."

"It was the right thing to do," she said as she slipped her hand into his. They continued walking up the steep hill hand in hand. Harmony looked down at the cobblestones under her bare feet, thinking that after today she'd always see Suijin in a different light.

15

Suijin was convinced today had been a breakthrough for him. Had he known Harmony would respond to his gift so willingly, he might have done it sooner. After he escorted her to her room, he went to his own to wash and change for dinner. Harmony promised she'd join him once she did the same.

Luna was waiting for him when he entered his bedroom. He greeted her with a wide smile. She stood by the window. The view encompassed the beach where he and Harmony had lain for an hour in each other's arms.

"Where did you go today with that human?" Luna's calm voice was low. She leaned against the pane with her arms crossed.

"Luna." Suijin crossed the room to tower over her slim juvenile frame. "I want you to be respectful and helpful to Harmony. She is more than my guest. Show her the same devotion you show me."

Staring straight at his chest, she asked, "What about us? Aren't I enough for you? We have been together a long time."

He lifted her pointed chin and gazed into her large, beseeching eyes. She was lovely, but she was a siren. He cared for her immensely, and she served him well. Many sirens served him well.

He reassured her for the thousandth time. "You are the best of the sirens." When the corners of her mouth turned up, he added, "But I want Harmony to be my wife."

Luna jerked her chin out of his caressing fingers, a pout on her mouth. "She doesn't want to stay here. She is already married."

He turned and waltzed to his bathroom, waving a hand at her comments. "She will change her mind. She might have already done so."

His loincloth dropped to the floor of the large stone stall. He turned a valve, and the spout above his head dispensed collected rainwater.

"Luna, come wash my hair," he commanded.

When she appeared, he sat on the stone bench so she could work the sand from it. She brooded silently, but he took no notice. His mind was elsewhere.

When she finished with his hair she ran her hands over the broad planes of his shoulders. "What else can I do for you?" she cooed.

Standing to rinse his dark head, he asked her to start a fire in the hearth, knowing Harmony would welcome the heat. Luna's small hands slid up his torso, but he captured her wrists in one motion. He bent to drop his chin close to her ear. "I am devoted to Harmony now, as I have been since she crossed the realms this summer. During our courtship only *she* will have my physical affection. Do I make myself clear?"

Returning to his full height as the water bounced off his taunt skin, he watched the hurt expression on Luna's face grow. Though she pouted like a child, she nodded that she understood he wouldn't bed her.

"May I dine with you?" she mumbled.

"Yes. In fact, fetch some fresh white fish to prepare for dinner. Harmony enjoys white fish. You may join us tonight," he offered as consolation.

Suijin was dressed in loose-fitting pants, his chest bare, when Harmony knocked on the burled wood door. He had been swirling the red wine in the glass he held up to the firelight.

"Am I interrupting?"

Harmony's careful attention to her appearance did not go unnoticed. He took in her hair, swept to the side and pinned behind one ear, loose tendrils wavy along her cheekbones. She wore a strappy sundress; its soft pink heightened her tanned skin, and the flirty hem brushed her thighs. Her lips shone with gloss. He vowed to taste the flavor.

"Not at all. Come in. Luna lit a fire for you, and I've opened some wine. Would you care for some?"

"Umm, yes—that would be nice." She padded to his side. He noticed her reluctant glance in Luna's direction.

He filled a second glass for Harmony and suggested they drink on the balcony. He wondered if she agreed so readily just to escape Luna. He smiled when she joined him on the bench outside. Billions of stars were their chandelier. He slid his arm over her shoulder to warm her. He held up his glass. "To you, Harmony...to your new life."

While he took a healthy gulp, he watched her take a small sip. Savoring the last drops of wine on his tongue, he dipped his head to brush his lips against hers. She kissed him back—for a moment—before she broke away to glance over her shoulder at Luna, who was making them dinner by the fire. *It's all right. There will be more time for that later,* he assured himself.

They talked about the amazing things she'd seen in the underwater world and the other wonders he had in mind for her to explore.

Luna announced the dinner was ready, and the trio ate around his table cordially. No one brought up the incident at the mud bath. Suijin did most of the talking, entertaining the two females in his life.

Harmony thanked Luna for the meal, and he read it as his cue to dismiss the siren. Suijin ignored the sulking girl; his eyes were only for Harmony. He refilled their wine glasses, and the couple moved to the nearby sofa laden with silk pillows. Luna left the room with dignity.

Once comfortable, he amused Harmony with tales of the universe. "After the blast that caused the earth to form, there came a time when it cooled. As clouds formed over the earth, it rained for a very long time. It rained long enough to fill our planet with oceans. It was during that time when the oceans formed that my life in this prison began," he murmured thoughtfully, swirling the wine in the decorative crystal glass. "I watched life evolve from the beginning."

"Wow. I can't imagine the things you've seen and experienced," she said, her voice heavy with wonder.

He shrugged.

"So you've seen dinosaurs."

He grinned.

She pulled the pins from her hair and shook it out. Harmony snuggled deeper into the cushions. "Gosh, thinking back to grade school, how many dinosaur names can I recall?" She appeared to think quite seriously on the matter, but her expression belied her playfulness. "I don't remember too many. It's weird that I'm here in an alternate realm with a god and sirens and strange mythical sea creatures, yet the thought of you seeing a dinosaur seems fantastically unbelievable."

He laughed at her amazement and confessed the dinosaurs had been menacing. Even though he was a god, he'd kept to the sea. She joined in his laugher, to his delight, and his heart swelled to finally see true joy on her face. It sent his mind wandering, and his instinct to possess her grew stronger still.

***

As time passed, their laughter faded. Harmony's eyes roamed over his handsome face.

He is so amazing...and so handsome.

If she had a lifetime, or even all of eternity, would she know him completely? She knew she shouldn't want to kiss him. At this moment she couldn't resist her fixation on him, though she knew she was playing with fire. She focused on his straight white teeth, but that brought visions of running her tongue over them. She licked her lips. She longed to be touched, caressed...made love to. Imagining his hands on her, her body tightened with eagerness. He was watching her, observing her struggle. To hide from him, she tilted her head to make a curtain of her hair.

She felt his fingers thread through her locks and shift her golden hair to the back of her neck. The pulse in her neck throbbed, as if she were a deer sensing a wolf.

Flee! Get up and walk away!

Instead she leaned forward, pausing so he could meet her halfway. But he didn't. This drove her crazier.

He was the one who wanted *her*!

He'd promised not to force her. He waited for her to want it.

Get up and walk away! Don't make a fool of yourself!

She'd felt so many strong emotions toward this man—this god. Could she resist a moment longer?

It's just one kiss...

She leaned closer, until her lips brushed his, stoking her inner fire. Her eyes were open when she pressed her mouth firmly against his. His irises were like sapphires. Kodiak's eyes were copper. *Blue is the opposite of orange. Sapphire versus copper.* How could she choose?

Suijin kissed her back, capturing and releasing her lips, teasing her with quick dashes from his tongue. Harmony felt like a sneaky teenager making out at a party, but this wasn't reckless fun.

She couldn't make herself stop.

He removed the wine glass from her hand and set it aside his own. She eased onto his lap. They kissed lightly for a long time before she tilted her head slightly; the kisses became deeper. His long tongue nearly swept the back of her throat before it dueled with hers. This sensual attack made her flatten her palms against his chest and twist closer. His hand slipped from her neck, and she felt him lift her hips until she sat on top of his pelvis, their mouths never separating.

Harmony's legs spread across his lap, her sundress bunched around her hips. Her palms smoothed the cliffs of his shoulders. But that wasn't enough. Her fingers found his long hair, and she played with the silky strands before she gripped fistfuls of it. Releasing his hair, she traced and explored every dip and valley from his ribs to the taut cords of his neck. She pulled back so her eyes could follow her fingertips. He was so beautiful to look at...and majorly sexy to touch. Her pleasure sensors were rising off the charts. She noticed that his scales were gone and was relieved she wasn't going to burn him to a crisp.

His hands slid up and down her silky thighs. One hand roamed to her behind, and a finger slipped beneath the edge of her underwear. She pressed against his mouth again, knowing it held her protest. As his fingers moved like a musician mastering the chords of his guitar, she inhaled sharply.

Her eyes on his, she blinked several times. She had never before seen the color that now swirled in his irises. A new color—just for her.

Okay, time to stop!

Her brain told her what she should do, but her body still rocked against his. He continued to touch her. Her heartbeat thrummed fast and loud in her ears, and her swollen lips returned to his. She felt out of control. His probing finger had awakened the beast within her, and she moaned against his mouth as she continued to rock her hips. She was close to a release that she desperately needed.

This is madness!

His finger was like a swirling tornado gathering every fragment of ecstasy her body possessed. If this storm reached its climax she would be lost! If she reached fulfillment…

Oh no!

Oh yes!

Suddenly she braced her hands on his shoulders. She broke their kiss to cry out as her body tensed around his finger. She arched her back and rode the wave until she shuddered.

She slouched against him, breathing heavily, her sweaty forehead against his.

That was a first!

His magic fingers had completely taken away her ability to respond with less than wild abandon.

She slid off his lap, clamping her legs together.

"I can't believe that just happened." she whispered, mortified. She lifted her damp hair from her neck, twisting it in her hands.

"I'm happy that I pleased you," he responded hoarsely. When he reached for her, she held up her hands.

"No! That wasn't supposed to happen! I was just going to kiss you. I can't believe I let it go that far." Her cheeks flamed, and she turned her head from him. This was her fault. She'd started it. Shame and regret filled her now. She'd let him touch her—and he'd satisfied her!

She was another man's wife.

"I'm going to my room."

He stood when she did, blocking her route to the door. "You're upset, but you shouldn't be. We are two beings who care about each other."

She looked up at him, wanting to deny his words.

He traced his finger down her cheekbone and said with conviction, "You know how much I care about you. I love you, Harmony."

How could she think straight as conflicting emotions raged through her? There was a fine line between shameful, passionate behavior and the craving to feel connected to someone.

"If you love me, then why haven't you let me go? That's all I've ever asked of you. I'm your prisoner here," she cried.

"You needed this time to get to know me. Now that you have, I know you've come to care for me. You can't deny that, Harmony."

"I know enough about you, Jin. And obviously I have feelings for you, but it's not going to work for us. I'm already married. And even if Kodi did leave me, maybe it was because he had to." Harmony twisted the pearl ring on her finger and confessed, "I still love him." Her voice was thick with anguish. She'd just betrayed her husband and admitted that she cared for two men.

"I feel so confused," she admitted. "It's not just my husband and the human realm—I miss my friends and my clan family."

"Would a life with me be so bad? I won't keep you from your friends and clan family much longer. I just don't know how I can go on without you. You are a part of me now."

She blinked several times. "I don't know, Jin. Maybe you and I could travel to the Forest Tribe's city so you can meet them? Maybe it's time to reestablish relationships with the clans and tribes. Explain to them all what you've told me. I would help introduce you back into their society."

"That city is far from the sea."

"If you want me to stay with you…if we could possibly have a future…I can't spend it in this isolated place." She pressed her palms over her eyes, trying to block out her confusion.

"We can figure something out, Harmony. Just hearing you are open to the possibly of there being an *us* means so much," he said. "Come to bed with me."

Her hands dropped to her hips, and she scanned his face. He wanted her in bed with him after what had just happened! She couldn't fathom his gall.

"I just want to hold you while you sleep," he offered honestly. "I promise to behave."

"It's not you I'm worried about," she confessed. She backed away. "Good night, Jin." Harmony rushed from the room, biting her lip and holding back the tears.

Has this beast become my desired salvation? Does he fill the void, a dark and stagnant place where my fears fester? Is he a substitute or more than that?

She knew the direction the unsettling answer was charging toward.

How can I love two men?

I'm doomed to follow in Calder's footsteps.

Calder had loved her human ancestor *and* his Aquapopulean wife. Nami, her aunt, had told her, "My father returned many times to your realm, and his health has suffered for it. My mother suffered, too, from heartache. The man she loved, who stayed with her and fathered her children, loved someone else. But actually he loved both women. He couldn't choose."

When had choosing between Kodiak and Suijin become a question?

16

Suijin stood on his balcony, mentally reaching out to sense the underwater life, absorbing the balance. For weeks he and Harmony had frolicked in the ocean. In that time they'd kept their hands off each other. Suijin realized he continued to earn her trust because she allowed him to whisk her to the far corners of this realm's seas. The hours spent leaping with dolphins in the waves had strengthened their magical bond. He conjured the dazzling smile plastered on her lovely face when she experienced something new and exciting.

When he'd made thirty-foot waves for them to slide down she'd squealed with laughter and splashed with free abandon. After listening to the concert of whale songs she'd nearly cried over the beauty of their music.

Now he glanced at the empty doorway. It was typical for them to meet for breakfast in his room before they swam off for the day. But this morning she hadn't come to his room. When he peeked into her bedroom, it was empty, which propelled him to seek her. After searching several rooms he found her in the great hall. He watched Harmony pick up objects from the vast collection of knickknacks that sprawled across the heavy console. He leaned silently against a thick column until she'd glanced over her shoulder at him.

"Good morning, beautiful. What are you looking for?"

She harrumphed and turned back to opening drawers and rooting around inside them. "I'm looking for scissors. Do you have any?"

He pursed his lips, wondering if he'd ever collected any. The sound of the drawer closing shifted his thoughts to other things. "What do you need them for? I have a blade if you need to cut something," he offered. He crossed the room to stand at her back. She turned, forced by his nearness to lean against the dark wood. She pinched a lock of her blond hair between her fingers and held it up for his inspection.

"I need a haircut." She looked at him pointedly. "It hasn't been cut in over six months."

He didn't respond to her time reference.

"The constant seawater is drying out the ends, and I don't have conditioner to tame this frizzing mess. So if you could find me some scissors that would be great. I'd rather *not* use a blade," she said with wide eyes.

He couldn't resist and reached out to caresses her hair. He pretended to examine it in earnest, but really he just wanted to touch it. The texture had changed. He asked, "Conditioner will restore it?"

She nodded. "I have some at my house, a brand-new bottle. Perhaps we could go..." Her words died on her lips when he scowled.

He stared at her hard. The silence grew.

"Never mind," she whispered with regret, snatching the wavy tresses from his fingertips.

"Harmony." His commanding voice compelled her to look up at him. "I will not only take you back to collect some items from your house, but I will show you how to cross the realms through the underwater portal. I will show you where the water is broken."

"Why? I mean, I'm really happy to learn how, but why would you show me?"

They both understood this could potentially provide her with a way to escape—if she could navigate to the exact location within this vast ocean. She would be able to do so from the Wellness or the Wentworth because the portal was just off their coast, but she couldn't swim so far from his island on her own. She needed his help to travel at his speed.

"This is in good faith, Harmony. If you choose not to stay with me and eventually return to your realm, I want you to find your way back to me when you change your mind." Although that thought weighed heavily on his heart, he felt diligence in this matter was vital. As long as Harmony lived, he'd be connected to her. She was his chosen one—he just had to convince her of that.

"So I'll be able to swim across whenever I want?"

"Yes. Now that you can hold your breath like the clansmen, it will be effortless for you." When she beamed with excitement he held up a hand in warning. "First you must learn to see it—the break in the water. It is tricky. Not all sirens can see it."

"Okay!" she squeaked excitedly. "Is it possible to bring others through it, instead of them using the herbs?"

His heart clenched knowing she must be thinking of the possibilities of Kodiak or her friends crossing back and forth.

"This knowledge is only available to the divine. I've never told the Linkers, who discovered a way around the bend using their herbs. The herbal concoction dilutes the atmosphere in such a way that they can be vacuumed through. That's the best way I can describe it anyway." He paused a moment before answering her question. "Yes, others can pass through if they are led by someone who can see the portal. I have little faith that either humans or Aquapopuleans are able to do that."

"I understand. I just wondered."

He tried to ignore her attempt to *not* look overjoyed. But being the source of her happiness hooked him.

"Can we go today? Now?" Her hands were clasped as if in prayer, and her cognac-colored eyes beseeched him.

"Yes, we can go right now if it makes you happy." He was rewarded with her beautiful smile.

When approaching the coast where the clansmen lived, Suijin regularly sped through the portal and was never detected. However, today he'd have to go through slowly so Harmony could discern where to enter the fold. When they were a few miles from shore, the land a dark bump on the horizon, he explained, "It will resemble a shaft of light. It's a very subtle crack. I'll swim through a few times first, and then when you see it you can follow me. I will quickly take us in by the shore. When I slow down you may see the clan's boats over our heads. Don't swim up."

He could almost see the gears turning behind her eyes. Knowing she wanted to escape him hurt him deeply, but it wasn't time yet.

"I won't. I promise to stay with you for a while longer. You can trust me," she vowed.

He reached for her hand and the couple slipped underwater. He slowed as he had said he would and showed her the portal. He crossed back and forth twice.

When his irises turned black he could see well in the darkest ocean. Now, in the semidarkness, he could easily watch her face. Somehow it didn't surprise him when she followed him through as though she'd done it all her life. After she came through he clasped her hand and they sped to shore, soon reaching the backyard of Harmony's property. Instantly he lifted her shivering form into his arms and dashed to the porch. He set her down and retrieved the hidden key to open the kitchen door, as he had seen her do before. Her blue lips uttered a thank you. She rushed in ahead of him and paused in the middle of the room, listening a moment. When he shut the door her guilty eyes told him she'd hoped Kodiak had returned.

Dropping her eyes and crossing to the kitchen cabinets, Harmony opened a drawer and reached for a clean dish towel to dry her face and squeeze the excess water from her hair. "It's gotten so cold here. March is always gray and dreary. I wonder what time it is."

"Late afternoon," he replied.

Harmony instinctually flipped the light switch over the sink, but it failed to illuminate. She jerked the faucet handle on and off several times. She released an exaggerated groan. "Darn it! They've shut off my utilities. And it feels like it too! It's freezing in here."

"Do you want to dry off? Change your clothes?" Suijin offered, wondering how long she would want to linger.

"No. I'll just grab the conditioner and a few things. I'll be right down."

When Harmony returned to the kitchen she stooped under a backpack that appeared heavy. She swung it to the floor. In her free hand was the stack of mail she'd collected from the mailbox outside the front door. She had taken the time to change into dry clothes and wore a thick sweater with her shorts. "Jin, I need a few minutes in the study. I want to send off the utility payments. I don't want the pipes to freeze," she added. "You know, just in case I want to come back and stay here, now that I know how to cross…"

He nodded and followed her into the study, shutting the door as she instructed. Harmony scooted around the desk and sat down to open the mail. He stood in the middle of the confined room, arms across his chest, looking around. He moved to the bookcase and gazed at the picture of Harmony's mother and father, the fishing vessel in the background. He remembered pulling Brook down to her death. She was young and beautiful then, as in this picture.

He questioned his fate. Eternally cast into these realms, why had he felt compelled to keep the realms separate and pure? He couldn't recall. The very thing he'd interfered with had brought the woman he loved.

Engrossed in thought, he didn't hear Harmony step up behind him. He flinched when she placed her hand on his forearm.

"Whoa, did I startle you?" Her eyes snapped on his face as she clearly wondered if such a thing were possible.

"No, I was just thinking. It's nothing." He flashed a white smile in the dim light.

"Okay. I just need this lantern to see the bills and write the checks." She reached for a small lantern on the shelf below him and switched it on. "Good, the batteries still work." She sighed with relief and then returned to her chair.

"So," she asked without looking up from her task, "what were you thinking about?"

Suijin dropped into the leather chair and stretched his long legs. He didn't want to dredge up her mother's death, especially because he was responsible, so he answered, "I was thinking about you...about your life growing up in this realm. I wonder how different you'd be if you had grown up with the Aquapopuleans, like Finn."

"Finn?" The pen in her hand stopped, and she nibbled on her lower lip.

"Mmm hmm. I felt him when he crossed with the Linker."

"Well, I wonder what Finn's life would have been like if he'd grown up in this realm with his mother. He almost came back with me before Nakoma followed us from the city and threatened the clans." She shrugged a shoulder and finishing signing the check. She tore it off and stuffed it into an envelope.

"Harmony, were you happy before you crossed the realms the first time? Before you knew who you really were and what you were capable of?" He had pondered this question for years. He'd watched her from afar when he caught a glimpse of her on the seashore. Leaning forward, he rested his elbows on his knees, fists under his chin. "Was this place truly enough for a woman with your talents?"

"What is that supposed to mean? Of course I was happy. My grandparents were wonderful. And I was going to college." She lifted a letter from the pile of fanned-out mail. "I haven't even had the chance to finish my last semester. The school is still waiting to hear when I plan to return."

"Do you want to return to college?"

"Well, I did. But now…everything is so complicated. Without Kodi here or Samantha…" Her hand snatched the bills she'd just neatly stacked; they were stamped and ready to be placed in the mailbox. She clutched them in her palm. "The Linkers should never have crossed in the first place." She blamed the source, as he had at one time.

He stood, his head nearly grazing the ceiling, and crossed to the desk. He said soothingly, "Erasing the past and your existence is unreasonable. You are a remarkable woman who can perhaps restore balance to the realms. Just look what you and Finn have accomplished so far among the Aquapopuleans. You belong in the other realm. And I think you feel that way too."

"What about Kodiak? He's here somewhere. I feel like I've abandoned him after all he's done for me." She sounded defeated. She stormed from behind the desk and marched to the door, twisting the knob, swinging the door wide, and disappearing through it. He heard her yell, "Shut the door behind you!"

Suijin collected the lantern and closed the door at her request. Turning toward the kitchen, he made his way down the hallway. He considered Harmony's answer, unconvinced she'd been completely happy. Even now he heard the obligation in her voice when she spoke of Kodiak. It wasn't that he doubted her love for the Diver, but Harmony was capable of so much more—the depths of her soul were profound, as only a god would know.

17

The coast of South America stretched before her. She turned to Suijin when he surfaced next to her. He squinted in the sunshine.

"Let's go ashore and find something to eat," she suggested.

"I guess I can't interest you in raw oysters or—"

"No!" she shouted playfully, cutting him off. She swam toward the shore. He'd offered her a multitude of uncooked ocean delicacies, but she'd gagged at every one. Now he just enjoyed teasing her. Harmony coasted in on a wave and stood in the surf. She adjusted her tank top and swimsuit bottoms as she climbed the slope of the beach. He strutted out of the waves right behind her.

"Hold up," he warned.

She turned to look at him. "What's the matter?"

"It's been a very long time since I last visited this area. The underbrush is thick." He glanced at her feet. "You wait here. I'll go in and find you something to eat."

She waved a hand at him. "I'll be fine." But she did glance down at her bare feet. From hardly ever wearing shoes outdoors, her soles had toughened. *I could use a pedicure.* All traces of hot pink nail polish were gone.

They entered the jungle, and Harmony wrinkled her nose at the steamy heat. Twisting her hair off her neck, she was glad she'd cut off five inches last month. However, it had grown quickly, and she made a mental note to trim it again this week. She inspected the foliage, hoping to spot banana trees. After a few minutes, she regretted her choice to join Suijin. Her feet suffered after several sharp pokes.

"I don't think we're going to find anything. Maybe we—" Frozen, she stared at eyes that stared back. A puma crouched several feet from her in the overgrown leaves. This cat wasn't like their friendlier feline cousins in the tribal city. The animal in the brush wasn't very large, but there was no mistaking its hunter's posture.

Cold fear ran down her spine, and a bead of sweat tricked along her brow. Suijin had warned her of the dangers on land and had recommended they stay in the sea where he could better protect her. It was too late now to curse her human craving for bananas.

She took a tentative step back, and Harmony's heart plummeted when she saw the blur of golden fur leap at her. Her arms instinctively crossed in front of her face as the puma's large front paws cut through the air. The cat's shrill, piercing vocalization sounded like a human female scream. Harmony closed her eyes and braced for impact, crying out. But all she felt was a *swoosh* of air moving the tiny hairs on her arms.

After hearing a thud, followed by rolling in the underbrush, she opened her wild eyes. Immobile, she stared in shock as Suijin wrestled the cat. He was a god of the sea—and this land animal was tearing him apart. He fought gallantly, but his bloody wounds left both man and animal slick with blood.

Hands shaking, Harmony scattered the plants at her feet, searching for a weapon of some kind. She tried to lift several heavy branches but abandoned them for a smaller one. With all her might she swung the stick at the cat. Miraculously it hit the bridge of the puma's curled nose, and the animal jerked back. Harmony released the stick with a bloodcurdling scream of rage. The animal's ears flattened as it skipped back a few feet. Finally freed from Suijin's grasp, the puma turned and dashed away, the underbrush rustling wildly.

Harmony rushed to him and dropped to her knees. "Jin! Oh, Jin! Are you all right?"

He lay still, his breathing shallow. The puma had sliced deep gashes in his shoulders and chest.

Tears blurred her vision, and she moaned his name again.

"I'm sorry, Harmony."

"Jin!" She dashed the tears from her cheeks and shuffled closer to him. His eyes opened in his pale face. His irises were the palest shade of lavender—the same shade as her pearl ring.

"Sorry? What are you talking about—you jumped in front of that puma and saved me!" She choked back more tears while she lightly brushed the leaves and debris from his forehead.

"I'm not strong enough in this human-like form to heal myself quickly," he whispered. She could see he felt the agonizing pain.

This is my fault! He'd altered himself so her touch couldn't burn him. After all this time, hurting him was not something she wanted.

"Turn back to your god-like state," she urged.

"I need the water to do it. Can you get me into the water?" he asked with a raspy breath.

She nodded vigorously and tried to lift him to a sitting position. He was a large, muscled man with mass Harmony could scarcely support—never mind lift. When he bent forward, blood poured like a river to his abdomen, pooling in the fabric at his waist. He groaned but managed to get to his feet. Harmony was crippled under the weight of him as he leaned on her. She staggered toward the beach, her leg muscles shaking.

He didn't speak again. His eyes only opened to thin slits.

"Stay with me. Come on, Jin. Stay with me," she urged.

They traveled about twenty feet before his knees buckled. He went down like a stone, taking Harmony with him. She howled as jumbo leaves smacked her face on her way down. She hit the dirt hard. The dead weight of Suijin's arm pinned her down until she shimmed out from under him.

She leaned over him, calling his name. He lay on his side, unconscious. *What am I going to do?* She nervously scanned the tropical forest for unforeseen dangers. *I need to get us out of the jungle and onto the beach.* Harmony stood to calculate the most direct path to the shoreline. It was maybe two hundred yards away.

Quickly scooting around him and hooking her arms under his shoulders, she wedged her feet against the damp ground and pulled. And pulled. Nothing. He didn't budge.

Next she lifted both his wrists, but her fingertips scarcely encircled half their circumference. She needed two hands to hold one wrist firmly. So she tried to drag him by one arm. Nothing.

I must try something else! She scouted around for something to drag his body on. Inhaling and exhaling to fight her rising panic, she thought about fashioning a stretcher from the jumbo leaves and abundant vines. She knew he carried a knife in his belt, and she retrieved it. It would allow her to saw through the dense vines. While she toiled to fashion a stretcher, the sun began its steady descent. By the time she'd rolled him onto her leaf bed she was drenched in sweat.

Exhausted and parched with thirst, she secured the vines attached to the bed of leaves around her torso. She'd never been a Girl Scout, and she cursed loudly when half the leaves broke away, but she managed to move him. It took all her strength to move his body several inches. She bit her bottom lip in frustration. She had no moisture left for tears, but she convulsed with emotion nonetheless. It seemed like an impossible task, but she was determined to get him into the water. He needed to be submerged to transform and heal. Otherwise she had no idea how long it would take—days? Weeks? With fresh resolve, she dug her heels into the dirt and leaned into the rope.

The moon was high when she finally collapsed onto the wet sand. The waves washed over Suijin, cleansing the blood from his torso.

"Jin," she croaked. "You're here…at the water. Jin, transform." She laid next to him, allowing the waves to lap over her. She knew the tide was coming in and didn't dare drag him in further, not that she had the strength to do so. She couldn't risk him sinking out of her reach. She needed to be with him to be sure he would be okay.

She examined his features in the moonlight and moved the dark hair from his brow. He was beautiful. Her fingertip traced the rugged curve of his cheek before her hand flattened against it. Instinctively she bent forward, pressing her lips to his forehead. With her kiss she willed him to regain consciousness.

Recalling his kindness to her these past seven months, even when she provoked him, she whispered, "I'm so sorry."

She kissed his forehead again.

In their time together, he had continually gone out of his way to make her feel special. More than that, when she was with him frolicking in the water she felt joy-filled freedom and a sense of being larger than life, using her abilities without fear. He offered her a life without boundaries. How much he cared for her astounded her, as did her growing feelings for him. Yet she still yearned for a normal human life with Kodiak.

Tilting her head, she touched her mouth to his, brushing the softest kiss across his still lips. Lifting her mouth only an inch, she scanned his face in the moonlight. It was easy to open the door to her heart under the darkness of night when he was unconscious and couldn't see her true feelings.

If she had never met Kodiak—if circumstances were somehow different—could she allow herself to fall completely in love with Suijin? It should be easy to fall for a man-god who cherished you.

Sideswiping further thoughts, a large wave rushed the couple, and Harmony lifted to her elbow to avoid being dunked. Suijin stirred.

"Jin! Can you hear me?" When his eyes fluttered open she exhaled with relief. Impulsively, she pressed a brief kiss to his lips before she searched his face for any sign that he was recovering.

His irises were black holes in the darkness.

"Thank goodness you're awake!" she squeaked, and she pressed another kiss on his cheek, her hands resting on his torso, away from his wounds. "Jin, you said you need water to transform back. You're in the water— transform back," she demanded in a shaky voice. Her hands left his body, and she sat back on her heels. She dared not touch him as he changed.

The waves seemed to have a positive effect on him; he moved again. He turned his head to look at her. "Harmony, don't worry. I'm a god. I cannot die." Though his voice sounded strong, she noticed his stiff movement and the furrow across his brow when he tried to rise on his elbows.

"I hate seeing you suffering! Just turn back. You need to heal!" she argued.

At his slight nod, she shuffled back so she wouldn't interfere. He settled back, his jet-black hair mingling with the sand; the granulated specks shimmered in the moonlight. The next wave washed over him. It seemed to gather rather than recede, and it lingered, covering him. He manipulated the water. Harmony began to worry that something was amiss. She waited with bated breath as the wave finally receded. To her astonishment, Suijin was gone!

Panic seized her as she scrambled to her feet. With a sickening feeling deep in her belly, she coarsely screamed his name. Her breath caught when she saw something in the waves. She realized it was his unmistakable, magnificent silhouette unfolding from the water. He strode from the water as if he'd gone for a leisurely swim.

Harmony rushed into his arms, pressing her cheek against his unmarked chest. An unparalleled sense of relief washed over her. Suddenly she realized she was touching him while he was in his godly form—and she wasn't burning him. She really was getting the hang of controlling her ability. She dropped her head back to look up at him. He stared at her with curiosity.

"I was so worried," she breathed. She searched for the color of his irises but couldn't distinguish them in the moonlight. How had she come to love his strange, shifting eye color? Her eyes rested on his chest and shoulders, where the puma had shredded the skin nearly to the bones. It was completely healed. She slid her fingertips over the smooth, tight muscles of his torso. She was touching a god.

"I'm fine. Better now that I know you can control your ability and touch me without thinking about it," he murmured gently. His hand caressed her cheek, and then his fingers lifted her chin.

Vulnerable and exhausted, she allowed him to hold her intimately. When his dark head lowered to hers she didn't fight him. When his lips touched hers she opened to him, accepting her raw, true feelings for him. She had been out of her mind with worry for him. Seeing him unconscious and defenseless—and all to protect her— had rattled her defenses. But she couldn't think about

135

that now. Right now she needed his comfort. Abandoning everything she was struggling against, she slipped her arms around his neck, drawing him closer and deepening their kiss.

She broke away first and pulled him closer, hugging him to her. He didn't question her or push her to kiss him. He patiently allowed her to advance their relationship, and for that she was grateful. Nuzzling her cheek against his, she inhaled his scent, the smell of clean rain. Secure against him and depleted of energy, she whispered into his ear, "Take me home."

She was swiftly lifted off her feet and carried into the waves. Her eyes closed. She felt herself immersed in water and then the pull of Suijin's warp speed until they reached his island.

Her home away from home.

18

Suijin carried his silent bundle up the curving road to his palace, moonlight glowing on his broad shoulders. Harmony was snuggled in his arms. She'd had quite an ordeal. He was thankful he'd seen the puma in time to stop it from doing to Harmony what it then did to him. His human-like form had challenged and weakened him. Perhaps it was unwise to permit this weakness, but it was worth it to feel her touch. Now that she'd demonstrated she could control her ability, their relationship could evolve.

When he reached the corridor he called out to Luna. The siren emerged at the far end of the hall.

She watched him with curiosity as he approached with Harmony in his arms. "What's happened?" Luna questioned, irritation lacing her voice.

He continued past her, asking over his shoulder, "Could you fetch a pitcher of water and some fruit? Or anything Harmony likes to eat. And bring it to my room."

"Of course," she mumbled flatly, obediently.

In his bedroom, he gently set Harmony on the edge of his bed. She lifted her fists to rub her eyes and breathed a heavy sigh.

Suijin slipped his fingers into her wet hair, digging to reach the scalp. As he massaged, he absorbed water as he went. Methodically, he drew his widespread fingers through the golden strands, effectively drying her hair. Harmony's eyes drifted closed; she seemed to enjoy his touch. Satisfied the wavy blond locks were dry enough, he took a moment to absorb the water from his own hair and torso, leaving everything dry but his strip of clothing.

Harmony's eyelids flipped up when he gripped the hem of her wet tank top.

"I want to get you out of these wet clothes," he coaxed. She lifted her arms in response, and he peeled the garment free. Her arms dropped and crossed over her naked breasts while he tossed the fabric to the floor. He smiled and reached for one of his discarded shirts. He slipped it over her head. She reached her arms through the sleeveless holes; the soft fabric pooled around her waist. His hands slipped under the shirt, and she rose slightly on wobbly legs, clutching his shoulders to keep her balance. His thumbs hooked her bikini bottoms, and he tugged them off. She shimmied out of them, and they fell to the floor. She stepped free, still holding on to him. He swung back the linens and guided her onto the mattress.

While he covered her legs with the sheets, Luna entered with a tray of food and a pitcher of water.

"Excellent. Thank you, Luna." He swiped away the clutter on the chest beside the bed and indicated she place the tray there.

"You are most welcome, Jin." She added, "I'd do anything for you."

He heard Luna's obsequious remark but was too preoccupied to comment. He poured a glass of water for Harmony and pressed it into her hands. He urged Harmony to sit up and drink, supporting the glass at her lips. When Luna's slim hand brushed his arm, he turned to look at her surprised expression.

"You've turned back," she gushed. She slid her hand over his scales and then said incredulously, "You were carrying her. Why didn't she burn you...or shield you?"

"It seems Harmony can manage her abilities. Isn't it wonderful?" He couldn't keep the broad smile off his face.

When Luna's brows drew together and she pouted, he chuckled at her jealousy. Luna's earlier words of devotion returned to his mind. Deciding to stoke her ego, he said, "Luna, you will always be special to me." Her features softened. "We had quite an ordeal today. Could you sing to us?"

Suijin observed the cold distain on her face when she glanced at Harmony. When her attention returned to him, her expression softened and she nodded. Luna moved to the stool across the room. She had often sung from this perch and did so now, her eyes trained on him. With Luna content, he returned his attention to Harmony. "My love, you need to eat."

"No, I'm tired," Harmony protested, trying to wiggle down under the covers.

"Just a few bites." He offered her an apple he had split into two with his bare hands. He gave her no choice but to take a bite when he pressed it to her lips. Begrudgingly she chewed with visible effort. After two more bites and a healthy guzzle of water she waved his hand away.

"I'm exhausted, Jin," she protested. Her eyes flashed across the room at Luna who sang a soft melody. "I just want to sleep."

He stood bedside, his open palm holding the apple. Harmony reached out to run her fingers along the inside of Suijin's wrist, ignoring his offering.

"Send her away and lie with me," she said softly.

He had hoped to hear such words for so long. He searched her eyes, wanting more. He sensed the barrier between them was crumbling. Suijin's heart soared with the idea they could become a couple—his patience had paid off.

He called over his shoulder. "Thank you, Luna. You can return to your room now." He knew his voice sounded more commanding than he intended. He should turn and apologize, but he couldn't take his eyes off of Harmony. He heard the deliberate scrape of the stool and the indignant tone in Luna's goodnight. Harmony's eyes followed Luna as she left the room before they returned to him. She seemed to study his eyes before a slight grin crossed her face and she rolled over to make room for him.

While she stretched, he dumped the apple remnants onto the tray. In one swift motion he removed his loin cloth, dropping it beside her wet clothes on the floor. He extinguished the lantern and slipped between the sheets, folding against her. He placed his hand on her hip.

When she reached back he worried she would brush his hand away, but she didn't. Instead, she clasped his hand and tucked it securely under her chin.

"It's chilly," she murmured as she snuggled against him.

It had taken him months to break down her barriers, and now he held her in his arms. She wanted him to hold her. He couldn't believe she was finally admitting to herself that she felt something for him. During the earlier ordeal, he'd seen that she was truly worried for him. It had given him hope.

"I love you…I will love you forever," he murmured as he pressed soft kisses into her hair and relaxed. Her soft curves were everything he had imagined he would one day explore. He was the happiest he had ever been.

***

Harmony woke with the weight of Suijin's heavy hand on her thigh. Turning her head on the soft pillow, she opened her eyes and allowed herself to lazily admire his profile. He looked peaceful in his meditative state.

Yesterday's tribulation had put her to the test.

How did this happen? How did Suijin know that if I got to know him I'd start falling for him? How does one love a god other than in a pious, devout way? My feelings are not in the least chaste!

What would being the mate of a god cost her? She would be altered—gifted with eternal life. She was already losing much of who she had been scarcely a year ago.

What about Kodi—my husband—who I still love deeply? Meeting Kodi in the Aquapopulean realm and marrying him to protect us from the evil Tribal Chieftain Nakoma started our crazy journey. I never thought Kodi loved me for real until he followed through the portal into the human realm. But those five months together in the human realm was a difficult adjustment for the both of us.

When she'd returned and discovered Kodiak was gone, she'd wondered why he hadn't left a note. *If only I could find him and talk to him at least one more time to discover for sure if he left because I didn't come back or because he wanted something or someone else. And I could go back now that I know how to pass through the portal—if I could only somehow cross this vast ocean to get there. But even if I had a boat it's unlikely I could paddle hundreds of miles by myself. For now getting to the portal was just impossible.*

In a year's time so much had changed in her life. She was no longer a carefree college student with high hopes of getting a job in Boston. Her plan to live in Bean Town and build a career as an architect was a shallow pipe dream now. And what about the hotel, the Wentworth-by-the-Sea, she'd advocated for? Was the restoration of the historic building progressing? Tears stung the back of her eyes. She was a changed woman who was completely out of touch with her old life.

I need time away from both these ringmasters of my heart so I can find who I am in all of this.

Just then her stomach grumbled, and she recalled her meager dinner of apple slices. Her stomach had gotten them into that mess yesterday; they'd gone ashore in search of bananas. She ignored the pangs. Luna had later sung a song about sailors and sirens. The wrathful lyrics seemed to be directed at her. She curled on her side, facing the wall, wondering about Luna's feelings for Suijin.

At her movement he stirred. Suijin rolled over to wrap her thoroughly in an embrace.

"Good morning," he purred into her ear. He stretched his lips to kiss her earlobe.

The shirt she had borrowed from him last night, large on her small frame, had worked its way up to her hips, exposing her bare bum. Suijin's groin was pressed firmly against it.

Her top teeth chomped down on her lower lip. This was too intimate…

If Luna could see Suijin and me now, snuggled like lovers, she would be livid. I've easily replaced her.

Luna is a jealous, vindictive little siren. Hmmm…maybe if I make her very jealous, she'll be willing to help me escape. Hmm.

Harmony started to formulate a plan as she wiggled free from Suijin's arms. Springing from the mattress, she mumbled that she was famished. She smoothed his shirt down her thighs and staggered backward. Half-walking, half-tripping in her haste, she reached the doorway and turned toward the bed.

Suijin was watching her.

"Sooo I'll see you later…after breakfast." When she heard her singsong voice, her forced smile turned to a frown as she realized how foolish she sounded. She raced away before he could comment. First, she planned to stop in her room to change. Then, over breakfast in the kitchen downstairs, she would consider how to get Luna to help her escape.

Yes! Escape is my new option!

19

May brought warmer waters around the island, but Harmony had told Suijin she wasn't up for a swim. She'd assured him she required a lazy reading day and encouraged him to take all the time he needed. He hadn't questioned her; he seemed glad to have some time to catch up on whatever he did as a god in these realms.

She spent several hours in the palace library looking for maps that could possibly lead her to the sacred island and her family. If she could get access to a boat, maybe she could escape. She ran her thumb over the lavender pearl ring on her finger. This was all she had left to remind her of her grandparents and Kodiak. Though her grandparents were long dead and buried, Kodiak was out there somewhere. She wondered for the thousandth time if he thought of her still.

She had convinced Suijin to allow her to return to her own room each evening, thus keeping their relationship in a state of formal courtship. Her plan to make Luna jealous had been in motion these past months. When Luna was in sight, Harmony would manipulate Suijin to pamper her, excluding the siren. Unfortunately, her well-laid plans hadn't gotten very far. He had largely excluded Luna anyway, taking Harmony away from the island most days, returning late at night. There were weeks when she never even saw Luna. Fed up, Harmony decided it was time to kick her efforts up a notch.

On this balmy May evening, Harmony found Luna preparing scented oil in the room off the kitchen where herbs and flowers hung to dry. She'd seen Luna applying the oil to Suijin's naked body on several occasions. Harmony whisked past her and appeared to hunt around the room for something.

She heard Luna sniff with disgust before she grumbled, "What do you want?"

"I was looking for mint leaves," Harmony said. "Ah, here they are!" She picked up a sprig, ripped off a leaf, and popped it into her mouth. She leaned against the counter nibbling it between her front teeth. "Is that for Jin?" Harmony indicated the oil, her voice casual.

Luna gave her a smug smile. "Yes, he's asked me to prepare it for him. When he gets back from his long swim he wants me to apply it to his skin. The water is harsh and drying when he takes human form."

"Hmm. He hasn't taken human form in weeks." Harmony shrugged. She added, "What about you?"

Luna sent her a questioning look. "What about me?"

"Well, is your skin dry? He makes you stay out of the water for a long time, and you're a siren, for goodness sake. Does he ever apply it to you?" Harmony's eyes were innocent, but she smirked inside at the look that came across Luna's face.

"I...I don't need it. My skin is fine." She cast Harmony a dismissive look, collected her tray, and walked away with a stiff back.

"Enjoy your time with that beast!" Harmony teased and then chuckled silently when she was alone. Getting Luna jealous was easy, but now she needed it to peak.

When Suijin returned from his swim Luna went to his bedroom carrying the scented oil. Harmony lingered and waited for the right moment. She tiptoed down the hallway and crept forward so she could barely hear the rumble of their voices. When she heard his relaxed sigh, it was her cue to barge in.

"Oh, I'm sorry. I thought you were alone," she said fluttering her lashes and catching her bottom lip between her teeth.

Suijin and Luna turned at her voice. He sat up on the table with thick woolens and linens draped over it. He wore only loose fitting shorts, and his tanned skin glistened with oil. "Come in, Harmony."

She took a few tentative steps, giving him her best reluctant performance. "I just wanted to talk to you, but if you are busy..." She looked pointedly at Luna, who glared back at her.

"Come. I'm not busy." He stood.

Harmony rubbed her arms and feigned a chill. Glancing at the dark fireplace, she said, "No fire tonight?"

"We can build a fire. Are you cold?" He came toward her and put his arm around her. She gave him a sweet smile to reward him for picking up on her hint. His arm was slick with oil against hers. She ran her hand over his arm.

"That must feel good. My skin is terribly dry." She moved her hand back to brush at the imaginary dusty flakes on her own arm.

"You will love this. Luna makes it special for me. Sit here."

Harmony wiggled onto the table and let the shawl that had been hiding her skimpy clothing drop to the table. The dress was made of the flimsiest of fabric; the straps holding it in place were no thicker than strings. The neck scooped low, exposing her cleavage. It flowed to her knees, but when she was sitting, half her thighs were bare. He looked her over as he opened the bottle and poured the honey-colored liquid into his hands. He rubbed his hands together, the friction warming the oil. Then he slid his palms up her arms, and her body shimmied with a chill.

"Oh, the fire..." he whispered, apparently distracted by her nearness. "I need to fetch some wood from the kitchens."

"Um, maybe you could send her." Harmony peeked over his muscled shoulder at Luna, who watched them intently.

He turned as though he'd forgotten Luna was even in the room. "Luna, would you mind bring up some firewood? Just a few pieces—whatever you can carry."

"It's not cold. It's late May," Luna protested. Her huge eyes narrowed like daggers at Harmony.

Harmony clasped Suijin's thick wrist; his hands had left her when he'd turned to ask Luna about the firewood.

"This smells amazing." She held his palm up to her face.

He spun back to her. She closed her eyes, inhaling deeply, and sighed dramatically. When she opened her eyes, he was staring at her, still as a statue. "Could you put some on my back?"

He nodded his dark head and stepped around the table. He shifted her curtain of hair around one shoulder, and she slipped her straps down with two quick sweeps. She rested her fists against her chest so the fabric wouldn't flutter down.

"Jin, I wasn't finished applying the oil on you," Luna protested with authority.

"Oh, I'll do it while you get the firewood." Harmony twisted to look at him seductively. "I'll do yours, if you do me first." She bit at her bottom lip again, knowing a smile might seem a little over the top. His hand cupped her neck and shoulder, the tips of his fingers resting on her collarbone. He seemed caught off guard by her request. His thumb pressed in a circle.

"Luna, please fetch the wood," Suijin said with slight irritation.

"Mmm, that's the spot. I have so much tension in my neck." Harmony turned to face Luna as he worked his magic on her skin. She peeked from under her lashes at Luna, who swirled abruptly and huffed away.

Harmony had anticipated her little performance would work, and it had—wonderfully. The siren was asked to do a servant's task while Suijin smeared and massaged Luna's handmade oil on another woman. Still, Harmony had to admire the siren's lack of fear. She could burn Luna with one touch. Harmony began to think the siren had a screw loose.

But thoughts of Luna were melting away, along with her ambitious plans, as Suijin worked out her pent-up tensions. She could only focus on the feeling of his hands coating, rubbing, and pressing...*Wait! I need to stay dedicated to the task at hand—making Luna jealous so she'll help me escape!* Allowing Suijin to continue touching her could derail her efforts. Harmony needed to figure out what to do until Luna returned. She couldn't afford to have him dismiss Luna for the night to pursue her. And it didn't help that she wondered what pleasures he could give her. Harmony concentrated on how she might continue to set the stage for making the siren's anger surge to the point that she'd do anything to get Harmony away from him—for good.

Harmony swiveled toward Suijin, tucking her legs under her on the table.

"I just wanted to say..." She hesitated. She slipped one strap back in place. Her thick blond mane hung forward over her shoulder, covering her near nakedness. It was necessary next to stop his wandering hands.

"I appreciate your patience with me over our relationship. Moving to the next level is a hard choice for me to make. And I just wonder...is it me that you want?" She glanced over her shoulder to make sure Luna hadn't returned and then tilted her head, looking at him through slanted eyes. "I mean, what about the other sirens? Don't you sleep with them? And Luna? What is she to you?"

A belly laugh shook his shoulders. His eyes twinkled with mirth as he leaned in close to her. "If you want me to possess only you, you need only ask me, Harmony. Sex with them is merely a physical release, but with you, the woman I love...it will be only you forever. Just ask me." The jovial twinkle was gone, and his eyes smoldered with urgency.

"Oh." That sounded way more emotionally gratifying than she'd expected. *He wants only me forever. Shit!* Her eyes flickered to the empty doorway. *Where is Luna? What is taking her so long? This charade is for her benefit!*

"Um, well, I thought Luna was like your mate or something? After all, she is elevated above other sirens and lives in your weird castle." Harmony's eyes circled the room, hoping one of her comments would keep the conversation going. She wanted to save physical contact for Luna's eyes only. She didn't know how much she could endure.

"Luna has been my preferred choice for some time, but when you came through the portal this last time... Well, you know what I want," he purred, his large hands on her bare thighs.

"Won't this upset her? Us being together?" Harmony prodded, attempting to remain still as his fingertips brushed the hem of her dress.

"I will send her away if that's your desire."

"No! No, I'm not saying that. It would be cruel to discard her like that," she said deliberately, wondering if he realized how careless he was when it came to Luna's feelings for him.

Just then Luna returned, carrying three heavy logs in her arms. He moved to help her, the air surrounding Harmony immediately cooling. He unloaded her small arms and placed the wood onto the empty grate. He reached into a large woven basket nearby and pulled out kindling. After stuffing some under the logs, he picked up two stones. When he struck them together there was a bright spark, and soon flames were licking the wood.

"Ah, there you are." He stood and presented Harmony with a lovely fire.

She slid off the table and gathered her shawl around her arms. She stood beside him at the hearth. "Wow! Thank you, this is so nice of you," she exclaimed and then affirmed her approval with a flirty smile. Harmony could see he was happy to do something to please her. And she didn't have to look at Luna to know how it all irritated the siren. She could hear the annoyance when Luna spoke.

"Jin, since we have a fire, shall I fix dinner here in the hearth?" Luna indicated the basket in the crock of her arm that held ingredients to make dinner.

Harmony watched his gaze flick Luna's way before he formulated his reply. Harmony worried. Since she was finally showing interest he might want to be alone with her. He gave Luna a tight smile, probably ready to offer an excuse.

Harmony spoke up. "So what are you making, Luna?"

Luna partially rolled her eyes, but Harmony didn't pay any attention. She was already on to her next act.

"Hey, Jin, why don't you lie down? I'll finish rubbing you with oil while Luna is busy cooking," Harmony suggested brightly. Already back at the table, she collected the little bottle. Encouragingly, she patted the linens, beckoning him to join her.

He stared at her a moment, hesitating.

Harmony tried not to show her angst and held her breath.

He finally turned to the siren and nodded his approval for Luna to start cooking the meal. When he turned his attention back to Harmony, she released her breath, a bit giddy.

This is working! she sang in her head.

He made an athletic dive onto the tabletop in one swoop, landing in plank position. His muscles bulged in an impressive display as they flexed for her enjoyment, and he slowly lowered himself to his stomach.

At the loud bang of a knife on the cutting board, Harmony jumped, snapping out of her mesmerized state. She flashed Luna a guilty look. Luna had claimed that she noticed the way Harmony looked at Suijin—and she'd been caught! *Just as well,* Harmony thought. *Let her think I want him and might try to replace her—all the more reason for her to help me leave.*

She tossed her shall onto a nearby chair. With shaky hands, she managed to open the oil. *Why am I so nervous? I can handle this. I'm just applying essential oil on a god. A hot, sensual being that makes my internal temperature rise.*

As she poured a small amount of the light, greasy oil into her palm, the smell reminded her of gardenias. She mimicked Suijin earlier and rubbed her hands together to warm the oil. Slowly she placed her hands on his skin and swallowed her trepidation. She felt her solo audience glaring at her from across the room, and she didn't dare look up—not yet. She made small swirls at first, her pressure light.

***

His eyes closed in anticipation of her touch. The weight of her soft, warm hands was superficial at first.

"You won't break me," he murmured, and he clenched his jaw, waiting for her to increase the pressure. He heard her take a deep breath. When she exhaled, she pressed down hard, drawing her delicate hands, forearms, and elbows toward his shoulder blades. He moaned at the sweet pressure. No one had ever touched him like this. The siren merely smeared the oil on in soft swipes. She was working the oil deep into his skin, his muscles.

"Is this better?" she whispered near his ear.

Suijin released an *ahh* in reply. He wondered if his touch left her feeling like this. Not likely—he hadn't pressed so hard. *Damn, this feels so good.*

Harmony brushed aside his hair, allowing her access to the taut cords of his neck. Her knuckles rocked between the muscles, and he signed in contentment. Her thumbs and palms inched down the muscle mass that flanked his spine, and then she moved lower to massage the base of his backbone. Silently he cursed the shorts he wore, wishing her hands would continue down. Instead her hands lifted. He barely opened one eye, about to protest, but she was pouring more oil into her palm. A satisfied smile tugged at the corners of his mouth.

Her ministrations resumed on his legs. Both surprised and elated by her skills, Suijin's body hummed with serenity. "You are very good at this, Harmony," he murmured.

I can't wait to experience what other talents you have hidden away.

Boldly she rode the muscles up to his gluteus maximus with both palms, one on each hamstring, then beneath the fabric. She pressed her thumbs against the unyielding flesh of his behind. The exquisite pleasure caused him to blow out a long breath.

"You can thank my college roommate. She minored in physical theory and massage. I was her guinea pig."

"That sounds like a win-win situation," he said as wicked images filled his mind. He heard her stifle a laugh before she released the pressure. He took the opportunity when she straightened to roll over. "Please continue." His voice sounded hoarse even to his own ears, and he couldn't keep the Cheshire cat grin from his face. Watching her touch him excited him, and he felt his muscles tense. One particular muscle was impossible to control.

Suijin had completely forgotten that Luna was still in the room, despite her loud preparations by the hearth. When she trudged over he tolerated the words she flung at Harmony.

"What are you doing? That's not how to apply the oil," Luna snapped.

Harmony set the half empty bottle aside. Suijin rolled up on one elbow. "It's okay, Luna. Everything she is doing feels incredible."

Luna placed her hand on his bunched shoulder. "I will do it!" The siren's voice was shrill and demanding.

"Don't touch him." Harmony smacked Luna's hand away.

He recognized jealousy. It wasn't only an earthly trait. The powerful god who'd sent him to these realms taught him that lesson. He'd understood Luna was jealous when he brought Harmony into his life, but he'd brushed it off as childishness. But with Harmony's seemingly furious declaration and physical rebuke, he felt a rush of excitement. *Could Harmony want me enough to be jealous?*

Though it was a glorious thought to mull over, Luna recaptured his attention. She bent over, clutching her wrist. Her skin sizzled where Harmony's hand had briefly touched her. "You burned me!" she screamed accusingly.

"Oops...I'm sorry, I forgot..."

"You forgot your horrid touch burns sirens! You witch!" Luna hissed.

"Luna!" Suijin's reprimanding tone pulled Luna's snapping eyes to his smoldering ones.

"She burned me!" Luna whined. She seemed to be looking for his sympathy.

He sat up. "She didn't mean it. She said she was sorry. Let me have a look." He held her arm and assessed the damage. He looked up again and noticed the women's eyes were locked. "It's all right. It does not even need a bandage." He'd seen worse. He grasped Luna's arms and drew her to him. Suijin looked into her eyes, forcing her to focus on him. "You're fine." She could only nod.

Luna stepped back when he released her. "Luna, finish making dinner," he said without looking the siren's way. He returned his attention to Harmony. "Please continue, my love."

He eased back and settled in with anticipation. His thoughts returned to Harmony's jealous behavior. It seemed she was coming around, just as he'd known she would. His patient courtship had proved valuable.

I've waited too long for you, Harmony.

He licked his lips. His vermilion irises were like windows into the furnace of his soul that burned for her.

***

It seemed Suijin quickly forgot about Luna when she returned to her work. The siren's eyes gave off a lunatic vibe, and Harmony wondered how far she could take this charade.

Maybe this game is getting out of hand.

Harmony collected a few more drops of oil and rubbed her hands together again. She couldn't bring herself to look at Suijin's handsome face. His stare was unnerving her. It was easier to pull off her charade when his fiery orbs, burning like flaming torches, weren't branding her flesh.

Touching his exceptional physique made her heart race. *He can probably see the pulse throbbing in my neck.* How could she pretend he was an ordinary man when he was clearly affecting her more than she'd thought possible?

She tilted her head back and shook her hair behind her. This seemed to invite him to fling out his arm to caress the edges of her hair. Strands stuck to her sticky arms, torso, and neck. She bent over his chest and spread her hands over his smooth pecs, observing every defined muscle as she kneaded. The pressure she applied wasn't as intense as for his backside, but because he was so big she used her forearms to cover more area.

The table was low, and his thick shoulders spanned the surface from side to side. She had to bend over him to reach both deltoids at the same time. This brought her chin close to his, so she turned her head to the side. She refused to look at him. Her ear hovered close to his lips, and she heard a low grunt when her chest inadvertently contacted his. Gritting her teeth, she felt the delicate fabric of her dress immediately absorb the oil. As if the dress weren't revealing enough, now wet and transparent, it clung to her breasts. When she stood up, sliding her slick hands back over his pecs, she couldn't help peek at his expression from under her lashes. His smoldering eyes rested on the clinging fabric; his chest began to rise and fall at a faster rate.

Her pulse quickened too.

Feeling brazen, she slowly, deliberately slid her fingertips over the ripples on his abdomen. At the low band of his shorts, she observed the thick bones of his pelvis. Her fingers continued gently spreading the oil around his abdomen. Mesmerized, she circled one finger around his bellybutton and wondered what it would be like to dip her tongue into it.

What! Stop thinking!

She used the back of her hand to tuck away a lock of hair that clung to her brow.

The glow from the fireplace cast deep shadows around the room, seeming as sinister as her thoughts. *Boy, it's hot in here.*

Her finger snaked lower and followed the trail of dark hair beneath the band of his shorts. When a groan escaped his lips, she jumped with a start.

"That's enough," he announced as he sat up. He gently caught her arm and drew her close to him so she fit between his knees, which now hung over the table. He whispered into her hair, "I don't think you realize what you are doing to me." He dropped his gaze to the fabric that stretched in her direction from his lap.

And what you are doing to me, she wanted to accuse. She shifted her legs together.

"Jin, our food is ready," Luna announced, and she waited. "Jin, you are on the table."

He nodded and released Harmony, allowing her to step away. He responded to Luna. "Right. Very good." He hopped off the table and yanked the coverings away so they fell to the floor by his bed. He pulled up three chairs.

Harmony moved closer to the open balcony, welcoming the cooler evening breeze. After adjusting her dress and collecting her shawl, she returned to the table.

Luna brought over two plates. She placed one in front of Suijin and offered him her prettiest smile. He returned it with a "Thank you."

Luna set the other plate down and sat in front of it. "You're welcome, Jin." She waved her slim hand at Harmony. "I didn't think she'd stay for the meal tonight.

After all, she'd said she only wanted to talk to you. Besides, I prepared one of your favorites. It's not really palatable to humans."

Harmony pressed her lips together at the insult, but when she looked at the gelatinous red thing on their plates, she almost gagged.

"You can have some of mine if you care to," Suijin offered.

"No thank you. I'm not hungry. I'm feeling a little restless, so I think I'll take a stroll." *More like hot and bothered!*

He frowned. It was obvious that he didn't want her to go. He sent Luna a disapproving look, like this was her fault. Luna hadn't been in the least accommodating to her, and Harmony knew she had been commanded to do so.

"Harmony, Luna will fix you something else." He rose from his chair.

Luna oscillated her eyes between them, disbelief evident on her face. Harmony could practically read her mind. Suijin was going to make Luna leave their dinner to wait on his guest. A guest she hated! She could almost hear the siren's blood boiling with anger.

"No, enjoy whatever that is. I'll see you later," Harmony promised him. She walked away, knowing he was watching the sway of her hips. She flipped her hair for effect before she left his sight, knowing her last sentence was the nail in Luna's coffin. Let the siren wonder what would happen between them later this evening.

20

The Forest Tribal City
The Aquapopulean Realm

Samantha tapped her foot impatiently. She smoothed her hand over her enormous belly and sighed. She had spent the entire day with the weavers finalizing blanket designs for the summer picnics she was planning. It was already the third of June. Advanced pregnancy left her tired, hungry, and thoroughly annoyed that her husband hadn't returned yet from the outlying farms. He wasn't supposed to leave the city with her so near her time. This baby was coming any day now.

She climbed the stairs to her chamber at an awkward angle; she could no longer lift her knees straight up. The baby had dropped, making that movement impossible. Amadahy, her room attendant, rushed up the stairwell behind her and offered a hand for support.

"Where have you been? The children have been asking for you," Amadahy asked with concern.

Samantha grinned as she glanced at Amadahy's youthful face. Harmony had been right long ago when she had introduced them and predicted they would become great friends. Not only had Amadahy's friendship squelched any loneliness Samantha had felt when she first arrived, but her loyalty was invaluable. And as for the children, she couldn't wait to kiss their chubby cheeks—just the thought reinvigorated her steps.

"Oh, I had to get a few things in order. Have they eaten dinner yet?"

"Yes. They just want to see you before bed."

When they reached the final landing, Samantha glanced at the pinkish sky through the bank of arched windows. From the looks of it, the sun was almost down. She hadn't meant to be gone so long. Her delicate brows drew together, and she asked, "Is Finn back?"

Amadahy shrugged a shoulder. "I haven't seen him."

Less than a year ago, Samantha had fallen in love with Finn and became the chieftain's wife. Now she was ready to give birth to his first child. Though her position as the chieftain's wife was highly respected, Samantha stood on her own merit with the people of the city.

The tribal women followed her fashion trends and were eager to take part in the human customs she showed them. She established children's programs, organized events, and brought the community together. The men offered her constant protection as their chief's expectant wife and encouraged her to put on skills competitions, which everyone enjoyed. The matrons heaped gifts upon Samantha and her unborn child. And the children were enamored of the human lady.

One sweet girl, Ren, whose mother owned a flower shop, brought her fresh blooms, sprigs of winter berries, or evergreen bundles every weekend. Soon other children were making her homemade gifts. Samantha made a humongous show of accepting the tiniest of offers.

Ren wasn't the only child Samantha became close with. Two orphan siblings had moved into their wing of the fortress and were under Samantha's supervision after their parents' canoe was sunk and their lives taken by sirens. After the tragedy, Samantha had cried for two straight days. Finn offered no objections to his wife's compassionate suggestion that they adopt the children. Though Samantha realized her hormones added to her waterworks, she didn't deny she immediately fell in love with the parentless little boy and girl.

Finn mentored a child as well. Bo, a farmer's boy from the same farm Finn was visiting today, was given the weekly task of bringing their goods to market in the city. Samantha thought it heartwarming that Finn took Bo under his wing. The boy idolized Finn. Finn's behavior with Bo and the two cherubs she was walking in to kiss goodnight reassured her that he would be a great father.

She entered the children's room with anticipation. The children's room attendant's face lit up and she cried, "Here she is!"

The four-year-old girl rushed over to hug Samantha's leg but released it to search for her hand. The little voice ordered, "Come see what we found!"

"They haven't stopped asking for you all evening," said the older woman, "but I told them you'd come."

"Of course. I wouldn't miss saying goodnight to my sweethearts," Samantha replied in a high voice. She eased into the chair and lifted the two-year-old onto her lap while the four-year-old bent over a basket and lifted out a furry white ball. She lifted it with two hands and giggled. "It's a baby bunny."

After planting numerous smooches on the cheeks and brow of the baby on her lap, Samantha turned her attention to the proud girl who stood at her elbow.

"Aww, he's so cute," she cooed.

"What is all this nonsense!" exclaimed an animated voice from the doorway.

Samantha looked up to see her husband's athletic frame filling the opening. The little girl inhaled in surprise but then ran as fast as her chunky legs could carry her toward Finn. In three easy strides he met her halfway and hoisted her, and the bunny she held, into the air.

"Have you caught dinner?"

"No! He's my pet!" she cried indignantly.

Samantha suppressed a laugh. In this world, rabbits belonged in stew. Finn shot her a look, his lips pressed to hold back a grin. This business regarding pets was due to her human influence. Finn claimed it wouldn't go over well with the tribe. Apparently she'd won over the children.

"A pet, huh. All right, you can keep it as a pet." Finn dropped a kiss on the girl's forehead before setting her down.

He crossed to the chair and bent to give Samantha a generous greeting. He gave her a few moments of his undivided attention and asked about her welfare. He passed his hand over the soft strands on the boy's head before he moved to kneel by the girl, who had put the bunny on a blanket.

It was in times like these, a Norman Rockwell moment, when Samantha felt the most content. She might have been brought into this realm by deviant measures, but this was where she belonged.

Later that night, after a quiet dinner, Samantha and Finn proceeded to the soaking pool. They undressed and swam in the warm water. Soon he stood in the waist-deep water, clasped her hand, and drew her to him. Finn's hands caressed her belly. He lowered his head, rubbing his nose in the valley of her breasts.

"Mmm, so beautiful," he whispered between lingering kisses.

"I feel huge," she pouted.

"I feel huge too. How about you feel it?" He flashed a wicked grin while guiding her hand.

She giggled despite herself when she felt him. "How about you feel this?" she teased. She laid back in the water and guided him into her.

Pregnancy may have made her feel less sexy, but she was still more than willing to be intimate with Finn. He was young, vital, and wild. He thrilled her in more ways than one. Besides, they were still newlyweds.

***

Days later, Finn held his newborn son in his arms. He hadn't known a time when he was this enormously happy. He couldn't express in words how fatherhood made him feel. He'd learned the meaning of true love when Samantha had come into his life. The need to protect and nurture his relationship with his wife felt different somehow from this brand-new relationship with his son. Gazing at the tiny face, Finn's heart squeezed with adoration, and he knew he'd do anything for this little guy.

That's what made leaving so hard.

The renewed search for Harmony Parker had already been planned. Finn was to leave for the coast in the morning. During the arrangement process he'd reassured Samantha it would be a good time for him to travel while she recovered from childbirth and doted on their new baby.

They both felt the weight of that decision now.

Finn sat on the bed next to Samantha. His adopted children rose to their knees to peer into the bundle Finn held in the crock of his arm.

"What do you think of your new brother, Parker?" They had named the mixed-race boy in honor of their dear friend Harmony Parker.

"He's so small," said the four-year-old.

The two-year-old curled back into Samantha's arms after a brief inspection, saying nothing.

"Right, he is small and fragile for now. So that is why I need you two to do something for me." Finn's tone sounded mysterious to their little ears.

"What?" they both asked, filled with curiosity.

"Well, I have to leave tomorrow. And I'll be gone for some time. I'll come back though," he was quick to add when their dark eyes became as round as mud pies. "I need you to look after your new brother."

"All right, but hurry back," the four-year-old agreed.

Finn locked gazes with his wife. Their eyes spoke volumes to each other. Despite everything he'd gone through, including being abducted and brought unwillingly into this realm to making a place for himself in the tribe, he had achieved everything he'd ever wanted. His wife, who he adored, and his growing family completed his happiness. Over time he even forgave his father, the Linker Gale, for what the man had put him and Samantha through. The only thing left to fix was finding Harmony Parker.

Last fall, when Finn had heard the news of Harmony's disappearance, he and a group of warriors had made haste for the coast. Expecting him, Calder had commenced making plans for sending ships to locate his great-great-granddaughter. If Suijin had her and she was still alive, then she'd likely be in his city. However, those coordinates had mysteriously disappeared centuries ago. Month after month, scout crews had been launched to continue the search for the island while Finn returned to the tribe, but nothing had turned up. After nine months of searching they had little hope.

Finn made a vow to Samantha that he would find out what had happened to their friend. Though their good-bye was agony, it was necessary.

21

The sea was calm. Sunshine warmed the flat rocks the sirens sunbathed on. Their feet dangled in the water. Luna had gone for an early swim with other sirens, and now chatted socially on the east side of the stone city. Luna filled their ears with new gossip about how Harmony Parker had burned her last night, pointing to the scar on her wrist. She was smug with satisfaction over their irate responses.

Images of Harmony in Suijin's bed haunted and repulsed her. She couldn't bring herself to greet Suijin that morning or serve him breakfast, knowing that mixed-race menace would be lying next to him. Fuming, she worried about other gifts Suijin gave Harmony to elevate her status.

Everything she had on this island with him was threatened and in jeopardy—just as in the past when Serena was alive. Luna was glad when Serena had finally died, giving her complete access to Suijin. He had quickly replaced his old lover with her, making her the envy of the other sirens.

The other sirens saw Harmony approaching. Luna watched their frightened expressions before they immediately disappeared under the sapphire surface. Luna contemplated joining them but wasn't going to let Harmony think she was afraid of her too. She dared not anger Suijin again. He'd spoken harshly to her, like never before, when she had complained about doing Harmony's bidding.

Luna turned her head toward the ocean, wondering if Harmony had come to gloat.

The golden-haired human jumped her way from boulder to boulder before Harmony reached the flat stone the siren was perched on. "Luna! I need to talk to you."

"What do you want," she threw over her shoulder.

"Look, Luna, I know you want Jin's attention back…and I can help you get it."

The siren turned to face Harmony, who waited, holding her elbows, keeping her dangerous hands occupied.

"What do you mean?" Luna asked suspiciously. She wanted that more than anything but wondered what game she was playing.

"My friends and family want me back. They don't even know Suijin has stolen me away to this place. You can help me—and yourself—if you tell the Linker Calder where I am. He is at the Wellness temple on the sacred island."

"Jin wouldn't like that," she asserted.

"No, I know. But he doesn't have to know it was you who tipped off my family. Once they come for me he'll have to let me go with them. I will be out of your lives forever."

Could Luna trust what Harmony said? To her, it was incredible that someone wouldn't want to remain in their god's good graces. To have the devotion of a god was divine in itself. *What a stupid girl.* Suijin had given her precious gifts, and she didn't even seem grateful. She toyed with him—and he encouraged it. There was no mistake Harmony had changed him. Would Luna ever truly get him back?

The thought of going to the sacred island among the Aquapopuleans didn't sit well with her.

What if they recognize me as a siren? What would they do to me if they caught me? What would Jin do if he knew I told them where he was hiding Harmony Parker?

Luna knew it would be wrong, but it was the only viable idea to get back the man she loved. She agreed to do it.

Luna swam up the New England coast toward the temple. She'd been here many times when Suijin came to watch the clans. It was difficult to swim wearing the vest-style tunic, the article of clothing she found that most closely resembled what the clans' people wore. She needed to attempt to blend in, though that might not be possible. She had the distinct petite frame and endearing enlarged eyes that were a siren's signature. She hoped the fact that she could walk on land would mask her secret.

Luna swam to the edge of the beach and crouched behind the large boulders on the rocky shore before she broke for the tree line. She saw the Wellness temple on the bluff, and her eyes scanned the port. It was a clear summer's day, when fishing vessels should spend the day out catching fish; instead they clogged the port. The largest ships she had seen in this realm dominated the harbor. The wooden hulls of the longboats were sleek, the oars propped and ready. Their tall masts pointed toward the sky like paint brushes, the sky above smeared with wisps of clouds. The tall ships were being loaded with a steady supply of weapons and provisions, buckets of arrows, and barrels, likely containing food and water. It appeared they were preparing for a long voyage.

Luna squeezed the excess water from her black hair and shook it out. She crossed the small beach to skirt the busy docks until she was forced to step onto the boardwalk and join the crowd. Barefoot, treading lightly, she listened to the movements of their sandal-clad feet and their casual conversation. Moving among them, she felt small and out of place. The steps hugged the hillside and led to the lawn in front of the temple. She started up the wooden steps, alert but keeping her eyelids downcast.

A young man descended with a group of other boys carrying baskets of arrows. His shoulder bumped hers as she tried to slip through the crush of people on the narrowing steps. He twisted to apologize and paused momentarily when he looked into her juvenile face.

Their eyes locked.

Luna panicked that she'd be recognized as a siren. She swung her damp hair over her shoulder and quickly moved on. She hastened, sure footed, to climb to each tiered landing that took her closer to the temple.

Once inside, her anxiousness surged. She felt completely vulnerable among the land dwellers. Never having stepped inside the temple before, she swept her eyes around the interior. A young woman stood behind a counter in the lobby, watching the activity.

Luna hurried over and leaned over the counter. "I'm looking for Calder the Linker." Her high youthful voice rang out, and the woman behind the counter hesitated and looked closely at Luna.

"He's over there," she said, pointing, still eyeing Luna oddly.

Luna almost lost her nerve when she saw the white-haired Linker surrounded by thick-muscled tribal warriors. As if that wasn't bad enough, she overheard Calder instructing them how to infiltrate the island town she and Suijin lived on. She realized they must know about Harmony and had somehow discovered the way to the island. They were preparing to attack if necessary to rescue her.

She needed to leave now and warn Jin. Before she could spin away and abort her mission, Calder caught her eye. He paused in midsentence, his keen eyes narrowing in suspicion. She turned abruptly, desperate to escape.

Her eyes were still locked on Calder and his companions. She heard the gravelly old voice call, "Stop that girl!"

The warriors spotted her as Calder exclaimed, "She's a siren—a siren among us!"

The tribesmen lurched forward, hunters instinctively chasing their prey.

She dashed between several clan girls who'd been smiling and flirting with muscle-flexing tribesmen. She heard shuffles behind her as she burst into the sunshine outside, the brightness momentarily blinding her.

I have to reach the water. If I can just make it into the water, not even the clansmen can outswim me!

Every fiber in her being propelled her escape—she had to convince Jin to let Harmony go without a fight. She wove through the groups of people outside the Wellness, as quick and agile as a teenager, her slim legs moving on land nearly as swiftly as if she were swimming in the sea. Leaving the congestion behind, her heart racing, she dashed down the grassy embankment and through the scrub toward the beach.

More shouts alerted those on the dock. Several men ran down the docks, jumping over the boards onto the hard-packed sand to intercept her. Her feet met the sand; her toes gripped the thick wetness. She sped toward the water's edge, and she'd almost made it, but she was no match on land against the men's long, powerful strides. A man tackled her, dropping them in the sand and knocking the wind out of her. Her braced elbows broke her fall. Her head turned toward the sea, she watched a wave crest and reach for her. Tears stung her eyes when it receded without touching her.

The weight disappeared from her back. A strong hand clasped her wrist and yanked her to her feet. Her ability to unhinge her jaw and open her mouth wide was the key to her escape. Her jawbone shifted, but before she could reveal the rows of razor-sharp teeth behind her eyeteeth, her eyes locked for a second time with the boy she'd bumped shoulders with on the steps.

He seemed to recognize her too.

They were quickly surrounded by the handful of hunters and clansmen who'd chased her.

A warrior called to the man holding her. "Rio, watch out for her mouth!" And he tossed Rio a leather harness.

Rio caught it with his free hand.

Another man was quickly behind her, clasping her biceps. Though she tried to twist her upper body away, the man's steely grip held fast. Rio released her wrist to adjust the harness. He hesitated for a fraction of a second.

Luna doubted that pleading she was just a human girl would work. Her telltale large eyes, flawless pale skin, and petite stature sealed her fate—she was marked as a creature of the sea.

It seemed Rio realized it as well. As her jaw released, she arched her neck to bite him when he placed the harness over her head, aiming for his arm, though she'd prefer his jugular. He managed to outmaneuver her chomping efforts. She felt the rough leather against her face. A portion of the siren harness covered her mouth. The rest hooked under her chin, fastened by straps above her ears at the back of her head. Her lovely wild eyes were left exposed.

From behind her shoulder, Rio asked the man binding her wrists together, "Finn, how is it possible she's on land?"

"That's what we're going to find out. Suijin is likely responsible. If she doesn't want to tell us then we'll just have to ask him." Finn pushed Luna in Rio's direction. "Let's get her on the ship. We are ready to leave."

Dejected, Luna allowed Rio to lead her. Even if she broke free, she couldn't swim with her hands tied. As they approached the dock, onlookers pointed at her, plainly shocked that she walked among them. She heard the commanding sound of Finn's voice shouting instructions, and she observed the people who followed his orders without hesitation. She assumed he was someone important, someone from the tribe, judging from his buckskin and leather clothing. But she wondered why the tribe was here in the clan's village. Suijin had explained there was unrest and that the two groups for the most part stayed separate. This was unmistakably a collaborative effort. What hadn't Harmony told her? What connection did she have to the tribe? Harmony had insisted that the clansmen were her kin, and now Luna felt deceived. Perhaps this had been a trap all along? Suijin had to be warned of Harmony's treachery.

She was detained aboard the ship while they waited for Calder. Finn met the white-haired Linker and they spoke confidentially. She watched them deciding her fate.

When they approached, she ineffectively pulled against Rio's grip. Her eyes shifted from one to the other, trying to read their expressions. When Finn stood in front of her, she quivered in his shadow. The sailors had referred to Finn as "chief." She recalled the siren's gossip about a new tribal chieftain appointed after the earthquake last year. Her eyes rolled up to meet his—he was a menacing sight.

Calder seemed a wise Linker, and he spoke first. "You asked for me, siren. Why?"

She glanced his way, but her eyes returned quickly to the larger chieftain. Finn waited beside the frail old man, his tree-limb arms folded over his chest.

"Harmony Parker sent me," she said coldly against the leather that scratched her lips.

Finn exploded. "Where is she? Tell us where Harmony is!"

"I will show you the way—but it sounds like you already know." She had heard Calder speaking of the island in the temple. "She is with Suijin and has been living in his palace this past year."

"The island—as we suspected." The Linker exchanged glances with Finn.

Luna shook her head, hoping to loosen the tight straps. She pleaded, "You can take this off. I won't bite you. I said I'll help you."

"She can show you the way, Finn." Calder sounded relieved.

Finn's concern contorted his handsome face into a scowl. He ignored her request. "Is she well? Has he hurt her? Why has he taken her?"

"She is fine. He has provided her with every possible comfort to woo her," she said with disgust, and then she added flippantly, "But she wants none of it. She wants to return to the human realm—to her husband. And I want her gone!" She turned to Calder and pleaded, "Take this off, *please*!"

Calder was lost in thought for a moment more. "So Suijin has found someone with unique abilities, which puts Harmony in an altogether different league and heightens the god's interest." Calder's assessment was correct, and Luna's nod was exaggerated by the harness.

"I will bring her home," said the chieftain. He waited to see if the Linker would add anything.

Calder appeared to be thinking while he studied Luna. He asked, intrigued, "Why can you walk on land?"

"I'm Suijin's siren. He will not like what you've done to me." The harness tightened when she turned her head.

Calder raised his bushy white eyebrows. Finn remained impassive, if not impatient.

"How long have you had this ability?" Calder didn't seem bothered by her threat. She wondered why the Linker continued to ask about her when his kin was the issue.

"Generations," she replied, hoping her many years with the god would mean something to these Aquapopuleans.

Calder turned to Finn and commented, "Remarkable."

Luna watched Finn clasp wrists with the Linker, signaling their talk was over. "I will do what I can," Finn promised.

The clansman Rio let go of her arm and said farewell to the chief. The Linker and Rio moved down the gangplank to the dock.

"Put her in the cabin," Finn ordered a burly tribesman, and he turned to shout to the ship's captain, "Prepare to set sail."

Luna, humiliated by the restraints, was tugged away and left alone in a tiny cabin in the stern of the vessel. The tribesman stood just inside the door, his eyes trained on her, his hand on the hilt of his blade. She took a seat on the narrow wood bench near the window, waiting until the fleet set sail.

Her hatred for Harmony was fueled by her annoyance that she'd come all this way and put herself in danger. Apparently their bold move to sail to Suijin's island had already been planned, though she had the impression they didn't know exactly where it was located—they'd planned to search for it. Now, thanks to her, they'd find it. Harmony had not lied that her family wanted her back—especially the chieftain, it seemed.

During the journey, she assured herself that soon the mixed-race menace would be out of their lives and she and Suijin could return to the way things used to be.

I hope!

22

Harmony brushed her wavy hair and threaded her fingers through it. She sat by the window, allowing the wind and hot July sun to dry it. She stood to return her hairbrush to its usual resting place on her vanity, but she paused and leaned over the sill to take in the panoramic view.

Her heart skipped a beat when she saw three ships approaching.

She had been searching the horizon since Luna had gone to the sacred island. Could it be true that Luna was successfully bringing her rescuers? Suijin hadn't even asked where Luna had disappeared to despite the siren's diligent attempts at keeping his attention. Perhaps he assumed she'd gone off to pout.

The sails of the nearby Viking-style long boats were bent in the wind. She knew they were maneuvering into the harbor.

At last!

As the breeze lifted her hair, she shook with excitement—and fear. Thinking about telling Suijin she was leaving created apprehension in her heart.

He must let me go—he must!

She turned from the window quickly, occupied by her thoughts, and slammed into Suijin's torso. The hairbrush clattered to the floor. She hadn't heard him arrive behind her. Her surprised howl further frayed her nerves. Suijin stared over the top of her head at the ships. Here was her chance to persuade him to let her go, but her voice was shaky.

"There you are!" Harmony said breathlessly. Even if these ships were merely a coincidence and had nothing to do with her, she planned to leave on one of them. "I was coming to tell you we have company. And...I think they may be here for me. My family may be looking for me." Seeing his dark expression and burgundy orbs, Harmony rushed on. "Jin, listen to me! Let's just go down and see what they want. *Please!*"

He rotated and strode from the room. Harmony hurried to stay at his side, jogging most of the way to the docks. He hadn't uttered a word. His face was stern, and his watchful eyes remained a deep shade of crimson.

At the base of the hill one vessel maneuvered close to the dock; the other two remained just offshore. Harmony clutched Suijin's wrist and hopped in front of him. He almost plowed her over.

She pleaded, "Suijin, look at me." She squeezed his wrist. "Please!"

After a moment, he blinked and dropped his gaze to her face.

"Don't be angry. Don't hurt them."

She could sense his distrust…and his darkness. Cold fear ran down her spine. He wouldn't answer her. Instead he moved past her, forcing her to release his wrist. She chased after him, her stomach churning. Maybe her plan wasn't such a good idea after all. Maybe there was a better way?

The boards on the pier were rough and hot under her bare feet. Several men were securing the vessel to the dock, but they quickly scrambled back up the ropes to the vessel when Suijin approached. She stopped at his side to look up at the awed faces of the Aquapopuleans, both clan and tribal members. The god's powerful stance clearly amazed all those on board. They had never before seen the water god. She scanned the line of sailors for a familiar face until she found one.

"Finn!" Harmony screamed, overjoyed that it was truly him. When she'd last seen him after his marriage to Samantha, she was supposed to be returning to the other realm. Calder must have told him she'd never arrived at the temple.

At Suijin's elbow, she turned her tear-filled eyes to him. "Jin, my friends have come for me." She slipped her hand around his scaled arm. "Please listen to me." She tugged again, trying to get his attention. Warmth surged down her arm, but she controlled her ability and kept the heat from reaching her palm.

Suijin, tense and still as a statue, glowered at the vessels. With a low growl, he drew his chin down a sliver and swung his eyes to look at her, but she could tell his peripheral vision encompassed the threat before them.

She was afraid of what he would say—of what he would do. If he wished, this powerful god could sink these ships with one rogue wave. Her voice cracked as she said, "Please let me go. I've stayed long enough. Jin, I've given you nearly a year of my life!"

"No. It's too soon. A year is but a grain of sand on a beach."

"Harmony!" Finn bellowed over the scrape of wood on wood as two men set the gangplank.

Suijin's eyes shifted to Finn and then back to her. Hers never left his face.

"Tell them to leave," he said softly, for her ears only.

"No!" Harmony shouted with conviction, letting go of his arm. *This is my chance to go back. I've paid my debt to Suijin.* "I'm leaving!" She wasn't going to wait around for another ride, and she needed to see Kodiak. She silently vowed to find him, no matter what it took. She twirled away and ran toward the ship.

"Harmony!" Suijin bellowed as he strode after her. "Harmony, stop!" In several strides he caught up with her at the foot of the gangway.

They both froze when a high feminine voice floated down from the ship's deck.

Luna! Dread filled Harmony's belly as she raised her eyes. *Why is the siren on board?* It was supposed to be a secret mission—she would give them the coordinates and disappear.

Finn held Luna by the arm. Her hands were tied, and a leather mask covered her face.

Oh no, Harmony bristled. *Suijin will be furious at Luna's treatment. Not to mention the fact that the siren is on an Aquapopulean ship.*

"Luna!" Suijin sounded confused...and something else only she could detect—hurt. He lifted his arm, the muscles tense and jumping, and pointed at Luna. He growled, sending a tangible vibration through the air. "Remove that from her! Untie her right now or you will regret sailing on my sea."

"I will do so *and* return your siren to you, but first Harmony must come aboard. I'm Chief Finn Falk, and I've come on behalf of the clans and tribes to take her home."

"Stay here," Suijin ordered Harmony.

Suijin mounted the gangplank and stood on the vessel within a second. Clansmen and tribesmen alike stumbled and scurried out of his way. The god stood taller and broader than every man on board. He paused in front of Luna and Finn.

Finn held a knife to Luna's neck. In the moment it took Suijin to disarm Finn and send the chief face first against the deck boards, he also fought off a dozen brawny tribesmen. He jerked out two arrows that were lodged in his tough skin. Blood trickled down his bare arm and abdomen from the wounds. He tossed the useless weapons aside and reached for the blade in his belt. After he freed Luna from her restraints, he bellowed at Finn, who'd rebounded to his feet. "You won't be taking anything that belongs to me."

Suddenly a huge spray of water broke the silence.

Harmony stood with one foot on the gangplank, intending to follow Suijin. She staggered back and focused her eyes on the spout of water filling the sky. Wrapped in its funnel, a gigantic sea serpent twisted and then crash-landed on one of the ships in the harbor. At first, the boat bounced under the weight of the creature. Then the splintering timber gave way and the boat separated into two halves that bubbled in the water like a lobster pot. The sea serpent rolled back into the sea, its pointy fins shredding the sail and toppling the mast.

"No!" Her cries mingled with the others from onboard the remaining ships.

He called upon the sea serpent in his anger! He'll never let me go without a fight. I must think of something—anything—to stop this!

As sailors struggled with their balance after the sudden waves caused by the destructive sea serpent, Suijin strode effortlessly across the rolling deck. He guided Luna onto the gangplank, and she hurried to the dock.

He knocked Finn to his knees, but Finn had already drawn another weapon. Suijin returned to kick the blade from Finn's hand, sending it skidding across the deck. Finn rose to his feet and scurried for another weapon. His hunters, recovering quickly, drew their bows.

Harmony maneuvered the wobbly plank and jumped onto the pitching deck. She heard Suijin's deep, rumbling voice.

"Tribal leader and half-blood son of a Linker, we need to get some things straight. No one shackles my sirens! And no one takes what belongs to me!"

Harmony hated hearing those words. *I don't belong to you!*

Her irritation grew as he continued. "Maybe I should have killed you when I had the chance!" The water god's voice boomed across the deck, but the fierce and loyal warriors closed in to protect their chief.

Her fists curled, and Harmony felt a strange electricity rattle through her. She shouted, "Stop! Everyone. Just. Stop!"

All heads turned in her direction. She shuffled closer to the powerful deity that stood between her and Finn. Her voice softened. "Jin, this is my fault. Don't blame Finn...or Luna. I asked her to go and bring them here."

"What?" he growled through clenched teeth.

Harmony watched the color of his irises sunburst to complete black. She shivered with fear. He looked like he wanted to kill someone. Although she knew deep in her heart that he'd never physical hurt her, she shuddered to think what he might do to Finn and her rescuers. She signaled to Finn to stay back.

Every sailor felt the tension; it was clear on their faces. And to heighten an already escalated situation, the sea serpent resurfaced. The monster swam toward the other ship, where men were pulling survivors from the wreckage.

"Jin, call him off," she begged, rushing to him. "Don't let it attack them again. *Please!*"

He didn't look moved.

She watched the sea serpent get closer. Heat snaked down her forearm. She squeezed her eyes shut and held her breath for a moment. She was too far away to do anything.

"I'll stay...I'll stay with you," she blurted, her lovely eyes glazed with despair.

"You care more for them than your freedom? You've changed your mind so quickly." Suijin's voice was harsh.

She hated hurting and deceiving him, but he'd left her no choice. She'd forced his hand—now it was time to talk him off the ledge, sooth this anger.

Another tactic came to mind. "Of course I care for Finn—he's my friend. But I see now that I made a mistake asking Luna to bring them here."

"She is a devil-witch," Luna called snidely from the pier, where she watched as the scene played out. "You should kill her. Kill them all!"

Harmony felt a pinch of guilt. She hadn't expected Finn to mask and bind Luna. The siren had done what she'd asked, though for her own selfish reasons.

Something must have gone wrong in the village.

"No more from you, Luna—you've said and done enough. You have disappointed me. Both of you have." He looked from Luna to Harmony.

"I'm sorry," Harmony offered in a breathy voice.

Suijin concentrated his gaze in the sea serpent's direction. Harmony's eyes followed his. Relief washed over her when she saw the snake-like body reverse direction and swim out of the bay before disappearing under the sea.

"What a waste," Luna grumbled under her breath.

"I will deal with you later, Luna. Return to the palace," Suijin ordered.

Luna stalked off. The sailors looked on with interest, remaining poised for battle.

The irises of Suijin's eyes were nearly red at the height of his fury before briefly turning black, but now they swirled to a dark orange infused with ribbons of bronze.

"And you!" He returned his attention to Finn. "Leave now and don't come back. Harmony will be staying."

Suijin clasped Harmony's hand in an iron grip. She was forced to trail behind him as he marched down the gangplank. Her mind churned, puzzling over a new strategy. As they neared the end of the pier, her heart raced. She realized that her best chance of getting away was about to set sail without her.

"Harmony, wait!"

She heard Finn's boots on the dock behind them. Looking over her shoulder, she shook her head at him, not wanting him to get to close. Suddenly an idea sparked. In moments it played out in her mind. She remembered Suijin telling her that he knew where all the underwater creatures were—except in the North and South Poles, where the ice acted like a wall and prohibited his powers. She stopped.

"Jin, hold on. Just give me a few minutes to explain to Finn what's going on and why it's okay that I stay...why it's okay that I *want* to stay. He's come all this way. Please, Jin. I told you he's my friend." Harmony moved to stand in front of him and drew his hand to her heart.

He stopped, searching her face, his irises cooled to a simmering umber. She couldn't help but smile, because from the way he looked at her, she knew he would do anything to make her happy—as long as she remained with him. Her hand stretched to his handsome face and caressed his jaw.

"A few minutes in exchange for forever?"

He exhaled in relief at her whispered words. He reluctantly let her go.

She rushed to Finn, grabbing his arm and dragging him as far away from Suijin as she dared. He instinctively pulled her against him and hugged her tightly, his words rushing into her hair.

"What's been going on? Are you all right? Did he hurt you?" Finn's expression was agitated when he drew back to look into her face.

She held her hand up until Suijin nodded and walked away.

"Shhh. I'm fine. No, he didn't hurt me. I've been here—and elsewhere—this whole time." When Finn released his bear hug and stepped back, she stayed close.

"It's complicated, and I don't have time to explain right now. Just listen. Is there any way you can conjure an ice storm that might somehow trap Suijin?"

"He can't penetrate ice?"

She shook her head and then peeked over her shoulder at the god who stood watching them.

"I can freeze the whole damn city."

"No, just the main tower first and then the palace. I'll arrange for Suijin to be in the tower while I slip away. This city is abandoned. You must sail to the western part of this island out of sight until later. Bring a storm tonight and freeze the tower at nine o'clock on the hour."

"What about you?" Finn's brows creased in concern.

"I'll keep him busy until nine and then find an excuse to step away," she assured him. When Suijin was in human form his godly powers were limited. She'd get him to change somehow. "I will get out. I'll head west and cross the orchard. Once I'm at the beach I'll swim to your ship."

"You're afraid of the water. I can launch a smaller boat to pick you up."

"No! I'm not afraid...not anymore," she said with conviction. "Can you do this, Finn?"

"Yes, but I need to be closer to ensure I can force enough ice to hold him. I will dock and wait for you— here."

"Fine," she relented. She flung her arms around his neck like she was saying good-bye forever, but she whispered into his neck, "I'll see you after nine!"

23

The nine o'clock hour was fast approaching. A heavy rainstorm had blown in nearly two hours ago, grating on Harmony's fragile nerves. Suijin had told her to stay in her room until he was ready to talk to her. He'd said he wanted to deal with Luna first. They'd been together for the remainder of the afternoon and evening, while Harmony paced until her feet ached. Harmony wondered what their conversation would be like. He'd seemed livid with Luna, but she didn't think he was capable of harming the siren.

Suddenly Harmony's thoughts took a different turn.

What if Luna confessed she'd been jealous and that she loved him so much she was willing to do anything for them to be together again—and what if Suijin is moved by that? What if they are making up right now? If Suijin is loving Luna right now…

Harmony wiped the sweat from her brow and swallowed the bitter thoughts.

Why would I care what they did?

She needed to focus on her mission. It was up to her to find Suijin and get him back to his room before Finn froze the tower. She couldn't wait any longer. Leaving her room, she crossed into the hallway and moved down the corridor calling Suijin's name. As she neared the siren's room, the door opened and Suijin stepped out.

"Yes, Harmony?" he asked, sounding sorrowful.

Harmony spied Luna seated by the vacant fireplace in the large chamber. Her arms were tightly crossed over her narrow chest, and her eyes were oddly swollen and red. Neither party seemed to have been doing any loving—probably more like disciplining and crying.

Why am I relieved?

"I've been waiting for you. Can we talk now?" Harmony asked in a hushed tone.

He seemed reluctant, but he micro-nodded before turning toward Luna's chamber and reaching for the door latch. "We'll talk more tomorrow. Good night, Luna."

Harmony heard Luna mumble in response before he closed the door. His expression softened when they were alone together.

"I'm interested to hear what you have to say," he remarked with exaggerated enthusiasm.

Several paces from Luna's room, Harmony glanced back over her shoulder. The door remained shut.

"First of all," Harmony started awkwardly, "I hope you weren't too hard on Luna. She only did what I asked because she wants you back—all to herself. She wants to be *Mrs.* Water God."

"No. It's not like that between us. She is merely a siren." The side of Suijin's mouth curled in a grin at Harmony's remark.

"Maybe not for you." She paused when they reached the threshold of his room. "I don't think you realize what effect you have on the females of these realms."

One of his thick brows arched, and he sighed. "Hmm, yet my effect on you is…?"

Now was her chance. She could tell him how she felt. After all, if all went according to plan she might never see him again. Once she made it to the continent, she'd go inland—far away from the sea. Instinctively she reached for his hand and stepped closer. When she looked into his aqua eyes she felt obliged to confess the truth. The very thought that she'd hated him once, when she was sure he was trying to kill her, made her involuntary laugh sound awkward and hollow. She recovered and said, "I didn't think it possible after everything in our past, but I've grown to care for you."

His lips twitched before spreading into a devastatingly handsome smile. Harmony towed him into the room and closed the door for privacy.

"I am so happy to hear you say that. Now that you've promised to stay and you've accepted your true path is by my side, I deem our courtship over. I think it's time we complete our union," he said firmly and pulled her into his arms.

Harmony's heart lurched and her mind raced. What could she say? His mouth swooped down, capturing hers before words were formed. His mastery made her legs feel like jelly. She realized she was clutching him, thrusting her tongue as greedily as he was. Though he'd taken her away from her home and family, he had also given her incredible gifts. She felt grateful for what he'd done while she was here. Her ability to swim like an Aquapopulean Diver had forever changed her life.

She felt him lift her, and she wound her arms securely around his neck. Her legs instinctively wrapped around his solid torso, and she locked her heels together. He carried her to the bed. Sinking into the soft mattress, she opened her eyes when his mouth left hers. He moved to lie beside her. He ran his palm along her arm, and it filled with gooseflesh.

"You're cold?" Suijin glanced toward the windows, Harmony eager to distract him. The storm raged outside, and the temperature was starting to rapidly drop. Finn was preparing to ice them in.

"It's your touch, Jin. You make me shiver with want." Her breathless words caused his dark head to swing back in her direction. His eyes, darkening like the storm outside, rested on her once more. She slid her palm up the stone wall of his chest and slipped her fingers into his silky black hair. She felt the blond lock of her hair woven into his as it brushed her fingers.

He moved to rest his hip against her. His finger deliberately, slowly, traced her lips. The dragging weight drew them open. He stared at her mouth, hungry. "You couldn't imagine how lonely I was before you came into my life. For the first time in the millions of years of my life I can say that I know what it is to love someone. I love you, Harmony."

She already felt frozen. Not physically, but her heart felt like it would burst. Her traitorous heart rejoiced at his declaration—and she felt wretched.

When had she befriended him? In the hours they'd spent together, she'd learned how fascinating the world around her really was. He was a wealth of knowledge. If she spent a lifetime with him she would never be bored. His devotion and care were constant but never too much. He gave her space when she asked for it. And though he told her he wanted her, he refused to force her—on the contrary, he seemed infinitely patient. She couldn't put aside her love for Kodiak, and she knew she never would. Still, she was experiencing similar feelings toward Suijin. She had fallen in love with him. Her throat burned with unshed tears.

"I have waited for you for so long," he moaned, his hot breath moving the tiny hairs on her earlobe. It was as though his words magically coaxed her legs open. She drew her toe up the scales on his outer thigh.

He's in godly form! Her eyes flew open.

She glanced at her wristwatch over his shoulder. Eight-twenty-five. *What am I doing!* She hadn't planned on a good-bye quickie!

She needed to stop this madness before it got out of hand—or, rather, into her hand. She trailed her fingers over the scar she'd branded on his chest while he sucked and kissed her neck. Her fingers explored the smooth steel plain of his abdomen and curled lower, over the fabric of his linen pants.

"Oh, Harmony, touch me, my love." He shifted, bumping her arm with his arousal. She swallowed hard.

"I can't," she panted.

"Don't be afraid. I'll be gentle."

"It's not me I'm worried about."

This curious statement caused him to lift his head and look into her face for clarification.

"I don't think I can control my ability while we're... You're not in man-like form... I don't want to chance disfiguring your..."

"Ahh, say no more." In one quick motion, he rolled from the bed to smirk down at her. "I'll be right back."

After he disappeared into an adjacent room, she heard the shower running. He was changing form. She was relieved, knowing his powers were weaker when in a man-like state. Now all she had to do was stall him a little while longer.

She skipped away from the window when she heard the water stop. It was too dark to see anything anyway. She glanced at her watch for the millionth time. Eight forty-five.

It's almost time to leave!

He stepped into the room, completely naked. He wasn't shy and had often been naked around her, but she'd kept her distance and mostly adverted her eyes.

Seeming eager and confident of conquest, he prowled across the room to claim her. His large paws landed on her chest, and he gripped the fabric.

"I want to see you. Take this off."

She hoped the heat she felt on her cheeks could pass as bashfulness as she squeaked, "I'm not ready yet."

He gently palmed her breasts before sliding his hands around her ribcage, drawing her close.

He pressed his mouth on hers.

She clung to him.

Her thoughts wandered, imagining them together intimately, rolling against the length of his naked, perfectly sculpted body. She boldly stroked his arms, missing the feel of the scales. Deepening her kiss, she almost forgot about the time.

A loud crack of thunder startled her, making her jump, which only made him hold her tighter. *That was Finn's warning!*

It's time to leave!

She clung tighter.

It was nearly nine o'clock. If she didn't leave soon she'd be trapped in the ice with Suijin. She wiggled to loosen his embrace.

"What is it?" he asked.

Does he suspect something?

"I'm sorry," she whispered between kisses, hoping to ease his concern.

"For what?" he insisted.

"For our circumstances... I wonder at the cruel hand fate has dealt us."

"We are together now. Forget the past. I love you, and I will always cherish you."

Guilt choked her at his endearing words. She was about to betray him.

"Jin, I...I'm going to go to my room so I can freshen up. I want our first time to be...special. I'll be right back."

She had to get away from him now! If she didn't, he would never let her go. Soon he would be encased in ice, with Luna to keep him company, although that thought gave her no comfort. If this worked, he might remain captive long enough for her to travel far away from the oceans. She might never see him again. Unexpectedly she felt overwhelmed. She hadn't anticipated hesitation. Despite her feelings for him, it would be for the best. But she felt so guilty about lying and tricking him. She wasn't sure what possessed her to dive back into his arms—but she did. She kissed him fervently for a moment and then pressed her forehead to his. With his face clutched in her hands and her lips brushing his, she confessed, "I love you, Suijin."

She felt a tremor shoot through his body, pressed close to hers, at her sweet admission.

"Oh, Harmony…"

"Just wait here," she whispered desperately and slipped from his grasp. She scooted from the room without a backward glance.

Long, shaky breaths blew in and out from the *O* of her mouth. Though the temperature was rapidly reaching the freezing point, she felt perspiration under her arms. Her stiff limbs hurried her down the hallway toward her room; once she passed the doorway she shifted into a dead run down the passage. The relentless run down several staircases jarred her bones. She shivered in the frigid, blustery air as she sprinted out the front entrance, but her steps never faltered.

I'm finally escaping after almost a year! I'll be free! So why is my heart aching? And why I'm I crying so hard?

24

The storm raged around her as she skidded to a halt. The air was frigid. A blast of warm air puffed from her lungs, appearing like white smoke flowing around her stinging face. She blinked back tears that threated to freeze her lashes together. The freezing rain pelted her and clung to her hair. Each breath was painfully cold as it entered her lungs.

She arched her neck and heard the rippling sound of ice as it formed around the walls of the palace. Shoulders at her ears, she winced at the ferocious cracking noises as she hugged her shivering body. Above her the wet stones thickened with ice until it looked like a glass fairytale castle.

Finn's ability to change weather never ceased to amaze her. Blinking continuously, her eyes swept the frozen surface, and she stared in surprise at the opening she had run through moments ago. Icicles now pointed like a medieval iron gate over the entrance door she'd thrown open. Harmony was mesmerized by the icicles that stretched like fingers toward the ground. How easily she could have been trapped!

Finn did it! He'd managed to encase a palace in ice in under an hour! He'd entombed the water god.

She needed to get to his ship. *Why am I hesitating?*

Suddenly a dull pulse shook the ice that covered the doorway. Through the distortion, Harmony saw Suijin pounding the now-solid surface with his raised fists. The ice had expanded to nearly two feet thick. She barely heard him bark her name in rage.

She lifted her palm to the ice but didn't touch it. For the briefest moment, making the tiniest step toward him, she wanted to return to him and apologize, offer him comfort. But she wouldn't. His rule over her was over.

She spun away and carefully made her way down the icy bend. The slick ground beneath her feet turned to black ice. Slipping inside one of the buildings, she rushed to a corner heaped with various items left behind by the Aquapopuleans. She reached to collect a hollowed-out sea turtle shell off the top of the pile. During her early explorations of the island she'd come across this piece and examined it with curiosity. Now it would make the perfect sled to maneuver down the frozen hillside.

The entire risky and reckless ride down the slick streets tucked into the turtle shell was terrifying. Boulders along the road to the docks loomed ahead. She threw her weight to the left, and the shell tilted on its side, scraping along the rocks, before it ricocheted her onto the damp sand of the beach. The shell toppled several times before stopping. She was sprawled on her back, but a dry heave sent her rolling onto her side. Memories of riding The Canon Ball roller coaster at Canobie Lake Amusement Park flickered in her mind.

Suddenly hands were on her shoulder, and a voice penetrated her cocoon of nausea. "Harmony, are you all right?"

She sat upright, ice and sand clumps weighting her hair. "Oh, Finn, thank god it's you!" Her eyes focused through the sheet of rain on the ice castle far beyond Finn's shoulder.

"It worked! Let's get out of here!" He pulled her to her feet, and she sucked in fresh, cleansing air. Her nausea subsided as they ran toward the dock where the ship was waiting.

When her feet hit the deck, the sails unfurled. Sailors worked fast to set sail immediately. They left the dock, and the vessel met each incoming swell head on. Halfstaggering, half-sliding, Harmony crossed the deck and clutched the railing. Her eyes glued to the palace, she felt the turmoil stabbing her heart.

"I'm sorry, Jin," she whispered into the wind.

However, she didn't have long to feel sorry.

A sea serpent broke the surface behind them. Harmony watched, wide-eyed, as the sea serpent skimmed and slithered across the ocean's choppy surface, racing to catch up.

"Finn!" she cried in warning, "In the water—the sea serpent!"

From the moment the sails had opened, Finn had worked his ability and filled them with strong winds. At her warning, he renewed his efforts. The sails strained against the force. But the sea serpent gained on them and soon rammed the ship's side. The monster circled around and knocked them again, this time splintering the bow.

She had to stop this deadly assault or all souls would be lost.

The blood pounded in her ears as her hands curled into fists. A foreign power palpitated through her, igniting her core with fire. The power was unlike anything she'd felt before. She dove off the stern into the churning black water.

The energy warmed her core like molten lava. Suijin had given her the gift to hold her breath, and evolution had given her the ability to fight sea serpents. With every stroke, she moved closer to the serpent. Remarkably she could see in the inky darkness underwater like never before. She saw its body zigzagging under the belly of the ship, its head thrust downward, only to scoop upward again, gaining momentum, preparing to smash the vessel again.

She maneuvered between the ship and the monster to send her force field straight at the oncoming sea serpent.

The heat that flowed down her arms felt different somehow, almost painful. Her energy surged from her fingertips in mini shocks, the feeling similar to when her stockinged feet rubbed across a carpet and she touched something that gave her a static shock. Despite the painful sparks that now traveled up the cords of her neck, she kept her focus.

It was working. She was forcing it away.

The creature broke the surface. In a manic attempt to escape her directed assault, it maneuvered around behind her. Harmony was its new target.

As they went round and round, the serpent trying to get closer and Harmony holding it away with her energy, the boat sailed farther away. Finally the attack ceased and the sea serpent, defeated, swam away. It soon vanished in the dark waters.

She knew she'd been underwater for longer than any human could be.

Finn must think I drowned.

When she broke the surface, she was relieved to see that his ship had turned back. *He is returning to find me!*

A sensation like a giant air bubble rose beneath her. Shocked, she watched the sea serpent rise, coming for her again. She submerged once more and prepared herself. As it opened its jaws, she forced its head to one side with her power and grabbed its horned head. Closing her eyes, she unleashed all her rage into the energy that passed through her hands. The serpent broke the surface and shook its head, trying to dislodge her. It thrust her underwater, spiraling toward the shore, where boulders hugged the land. She realized it planned to ram the rocks, likely killing them both.

Another painful sizzle of concentrated energy jolted through her into her hands. Just shy of the rocks, the sea serpent reared its head, propelling them twenty feet into the air. It bellowed in pain as its flesh burned, the cinders blowing away with the wind.

While she was suspended two stories above the water time seemed to stand still. The air that had been howling with freezing rain had somehow become tropical when she was underwater. The air around her steamed into vast clouds. All Harmony could see was the charred carcass of the animal she held by the horns. When the horns started to crumble in her palms, she released the beast and felt herself plummet down toward the gloomy water. The sea serpent's body listed to the side and dropped like a felled tree. Its large smoking head landed with a thud on the beach. Harmony dropped safely into the surf.

When she marched free of the waves onto the beach, Suijin stood there waiting for her. Harmony's eyes widened and she looked frantically at the castle—all the ice was gone!

Suijin is free!

She'd killed his sea serpent. She knew he had felt it. But she wasn't sorry. Breathing heavily, she prepared herself for his anger, but his face was a mask of shock.

Why is he looking at me so strangely?

At first, she didn't understand. But when she moved her sore neck to relieve the tension, something felt odd. She placed her fingers on her throat. Harmony tried to understand what she felt there.

Scales?

25

Confounded, Suijin stared at the woman before him. Huffing from excursion and standing over the dead sea serpent, Harmony had never looked more beautiful. The sight only confirmed that she was *the one* for him. There was no one equal to him in the earthly realms, but now she was similar. The gods had finally granted him a gift—a partner for eternity. However, he could see the look of horror on her face at this alteration. Perhaps she would still need some convincing. She had confessed her love for him. But he wondered what parameters she would put on it. After all, her profession of love had immediately been followed by betrayal.

He had to admit her plan to imprison him in ice wasn't an altogether bad one. She had obviously listened and tucked away personal information he had shared with her. That day long ago when he had taken her to her house in the human realm, he'd confessed he sensed Kodiak was still in that realm but far away. And he'd once confided that he couldn't sense other underwater creatures through ice; nor could he break ice with his abilities.

The fatal flaw in her plan, which she hadn't counted on, was that he could still summon the water—warm tropical water from the equator. Harmony had completely and successfully distracted him with her passionate kisses and embraces and the promise of more to come.

Moments after she'd slipped from his room, Luna had appeared in the open doorway.

"What is happening!" she had cried in anguish.

"Harmony and I—"

"No!" She cut off his words and crossed the room. "What is happening *outside*?"

He was beside her at the window in a moment. He had closed the shutters earlier when the rain started to keep Harmony comfortable. He tried to push one open now, but it wouldn't budge.

"Ice is forming on the outside of the palace! Come to my room. I'll show you." Luna never bothered to shutter her windows because the elements didn't disturb her.

At the mention of ice, everything made sense to him. He recalled what he'd once told Harmony. And he guessed her weather-altering friend Finn had remained nearby. Her minutes alone with Finn, when she hugged him good-bye, were a ploy to pull off this treachery.

Instead of following Luna to her room, he sped down the corridor in search of Harmony. He was too late. When he found her, she was already on the other side of the ice. He had pounded on the frozen wall, calling her name. Hurt and disappointed, he couldn't fathom why she had turned and run away. Why did she reject him—a god—when he offered her the worlds?

So he had summoned the warm waters, conjuring a tsunami, tall and narrow, to drench the palace. The ice rapidly melted away, like an ice cube in a sauna.

He'd shouldered through the remaining shards of ice around the doorframe and barreled to the beach. He could sense the sea serpent's presence and its struggle. Before the sea serpent broke with surface with Harmony mounted on its horned head, Suijin had felt its anguish. And soon after, he felt the beast's pain from the torturous burns.

He regretted the animal's demise.

He regretted that Harmony had murdered the beast.

However, he rejoiced when Harmony emerged adorned with shimmering scales.

He had stared in pure joy.

Harmony frantically yanked aside the sodden collar of her shirt, her eyes wild as she tried to determine how far spread the scales were. She gave up struggling with the wet fabric and tugged the shirt over her head. She dropped it at her feet. The narrow straps of her tank top allowed full view of the iridescent scales that traveled from behind her ears to her collarbone; the strip widened from two inches to four inches over the curve of her shoulder and down the backs of her arms to her wrists.

Suijin watched in dread as she wildly shook her head.

"Noooo!" Her tortured howl was followed by a low sob.

He stepped forward, his heart wrenching.

"I'm a monster!" she cried.

"Never say that!" His booming voice startled her, and she snapped her head to look up at him. "You are the woman I love. And for whatever reason, you've been altered—you must learn to embrace it."

Her eyes, swimming with tears and accusations, focused on him. "Did you do this to me?"

His expression earnest, he replied, "No. This gift is beyond my capabilities."

Suijin heard her name being called. He glanced over her head to see Finn racing up the beach. She apparently heard it too. To his surprise, she dropped her head back, closed her eyes, and released a heavy sigh.

Finn came to a halt a safe distance away. He called cautiously, "Harmony, are you all right?"

She straightened her head and gave Suijin a warning look. He noticed the tears were gone, replaced by shards of stone. He'd never seen this hardness in her. Where had she gone? He feared the changes were more than skin deep.

She must hate me.

Harmony turned and walked slowly toward Finn, who shifted nervously. Suijin watched shock and confusion move across Finn's face. He couldn't hear what the pair said, but Finn seemed argumentative.

It was all Suijin could do not to punish the chieftain for freezing his palace. But he knew it had been Harmony's plan. She had schemed all of it…manipulating Luna to go for help, manipulating him with her words of love, only to trick him into staying in the palace while she escaped.

I should be angry with you, Harmony. Punish you! He thought with resentment. But he wished more than anything for her to *want* to stay with him, to choose him of her own free will.

After everything that had transpired, he felt a sense of defeat. How else could he convince her?

Suijin's focus returned to the friends. Finn stood rigidly, his fists on his hips. Her back to Suijin, Harmony threw both hands up for emphasis. Suddenly she spun around, leaving Finn staring after her. Her eyes were downcast as she approached Suijin. She walked past him without looking at him.

"Let's return to the palace. Finn is leaving," she said solemnly.

Suijin cast one last glance at Finn. The tribal chief kicked the sand, scattering a cloud of it, before turning and marching back down the beach.

***

Finn stood on the stern looking back at the island under the moonlight. With a rippling movement from his fingers he sent the rain clouds scattering along the horizon. He ran his hand through his hair in frustration.

How is it I am leaving without her?

Their plan had been working. Miraculously, he'd pulled off freezing a damn fortress. After Harmony had made it out and was onboard, he'd thought they were safe. They'd underestimated the god's ultimate power.

They had gone up against the almighty—and the almighty won.

Fists on hips and a deep crease in his brow, he replayed the scene in his mind. The skilled sailors had barely managed to dock the ship in the enormous rogue wave swells. Finn hadn't waited for the gangplank to be lowered; instead he climbed down as far as he could and jumped the rest of the way to the pier. He'd sprinted off the pier just as the sea serpent's thud shook the ground. He'd run up the beach and seen both Harmony and the water god. He had hurried to her aid, not knowing what to expect. Never would he have expected Harmony to change her mind about going with him.

"I can't just leave you here! We've been searching for you for almost a year. What will I tell Samantha?" he'd asked her when she said she wasn't going with him.

"Finn, look at me," she said gravely, indicating the shiny new scales. "This changes everything! I'm a different…person?…species?"

"None of that matters, Harmony. You and I both know that!"

"You don't understand—this entire night I've had new and strange feelings, like something was taking over my abilities every time I used them… They were changing me. Changing me into a monsterrr." Her voice broke.

She stepped back when he'd reached to comfort her. Holding up her hands to ward him off, she took a deep breath and seemed to regain control. "So much about me has changed this past year. And I finally realize what Suijin has been trying to tell me all along."

"You don't have to stay with him. What about Kodiak?" He tossed his arms in the air. Finn hadn't always gotten along with the guy, but he knew Kodiak loved Harmony; he'd jeopardized his life by crossing the realms to be with her.

"I can't go back to him like this...not yet. I'm sorry, Finn, but I know what I have to do. I've adapted thus far, and I will again. I just need time to learn about myself, and Suijin is the only one who can teach me." Harmony's voice softened, and she indicated the god that intently watched them. "He's kind to me, and I care about him. Tell Sam and my family I'm okay and that they will see me again someday. I promise." A slight smile lifted the corners of her mouth. "I want to meet your family one day."

"I have a son." At least he could share this happy news with her. "His name is Parker."

Tears brightened her eyes when he told her the baby's name. "Go home to your wife and son, Finn." Then she turned and walked away.

He knew there was no changing her mind...and he hated himself for his failure to persuade her.

26

Rivets of water washed down the city gutters. The tsunami wave combined with melted ice caused the darkness around her to steam. Harmony looked beyond the hollow shops at the ship's starboard light as she marched toward the palace. The sound of swirling water made her glance back to the beach below. There were only stars and moonlight to illuminate the night, yet she could see perfectly well. Suijin had drawn a whirlpool around the scorched body of the sea serpent to lift the carcass and pull it into the ocean to its final resting place.

She'd killed a sea serpent with her bare hands—and spectacular ability. She'd had no choice. It had smashed one ship to fragments already. Finn had reported four dead and several injured. He'd sent the second ship home with the survivors while his ship waited to rescue her. When she'd seen the sea serpent coming at them—at Finn's ship—there was no question of not stopping it. She wouldn't allow the crew to be harmed. If anything happened to Finn, Samantha would never forgive her.

Harmony wondered if Kodiak would ever want her back after this complication. She was willing to risk everything to find out, but the only way she could face him was to be comfortable and confident in herself. She had to come into her power, accepting who she was and what she was capable of. She must embrace her inner monster. Only then could she search for her true love.

She realized she could leave Suijin if she wanted—not just by boat—but of her own accord. Not only was her eyesight altered, her ability to maneuver in the water had also changed. She felt confident she could swim to the portal now. She had become powerful but realized she must learn to hone the skills that were useful. She needed Suijin to teach her.

She crossed the entryway, the stone floor soaking wet. As if the tasks ahead of her weren't tricky enough, another obstacle stood in her way.

Luna.

The siren glared at her.

Suijin entered the palace; with one look, he sent the siren from the room.

Harmony faced him, her hands still rubbing the unfamiliar texture on her neck. "You once said a year was like a grain of sand, a short time for you, right?" She couldn't fathom eternal life.

"Yes," he agreed with a shrug.

"Well, then a hundred years couldn't feel much longer?"

He shrugged again.

"I have a proposal for you."

"I'm listening."

"If you still want me to be your mate—"

"I do," he interrupted emphatically.

Her heart pulsed at his quick and certain answer. "I would like you to gift me eternal life as your mate and teach me all the potential you see in me." She watched the corners of his mouth curl up and the light beam from his eyes like fireworks in the night sky. Rushing on before he became too excited, she added, "But first I want a hundred years, a lifetime really. I want to spend a lifetime with Kodi and then after…" She couldn't say "after my husband passes" or "after I've grieved," so she said, "When I'm ready, I'll come back to you. At that time you can extend my life—I want to grow old and gray with him."

"No."

Her heart sank. He would begrudge her happiness?

"No. You must leave here after I grant you eternal life. I cannot risk you dying from an accident or illness. I cannot bring back the dead."

"What? You agree?"

"I would wait an eternity for you." He cupped her cheek. "You are the only woman I will ever love."

"What about the sirens or the goddess?" Her question was in jest, but the humor didn't reach her eyes.

"No!" he exclaimed with anguish. "No one has captured my heart like you. And I don't want you to feel guilty about returning to your husband. Though you are altered, you will always remain part human and part Aquapopulean. I understand your connection with Kodiak and with the clan. For now, it is enough to know that you love me and that you promise we will be reunited again."

As elated as she was about seeing Kodiak again, she felt just as awful leaving Suijin.

27

Harmony focused on the bouquet of pale pink peonies she held in her hand. Light filled the room, and she glanced past the floral curtains at the sea beyond the window frame.

"This bridal suite is elegant...timeless."

Harmony swiveled her head at the sound of a feminine voice. The girl, whom she didn't recognize, wore a formal pastel pink bride's maid dress, and her expression as she glanced around the room was wistful. Harmony's eyes followed hers.

The walls were covered in a striped cream-on-cream wallpaper that coordinated with the cream-colored Victorian furniture. There was no bed; instead, a gilded trifold screen with triple mirrors dominated the room. When Harmony caught sight of the bride in the mirror she paused in confusion.

She was the bride!

Clenching her hand, her palm tightened around the bouquet she held. The heeled shoes felt heavy as they propelled her across the patterned carpet. She stood at the mirror, taking in the image before her. The gauzy white dress she wore was voluminous. Her golden hair was pulled up and studded with diamond clips. Turning her head slightly, she noticed the sheer veil covering her styled bun; the delicate fabric cascaded to the floor.

Though the dress and the room were strange sights to take in, what caused her the most distress were the scales that framed her neck and spread out over her collarbones. Harmony's fingers brushed the scales. She stepped even closer to the mirror, forgetting her surroundings.

The girl tapped her shoulder and said, "You look

beautiful. Wait until he sees you!" The girl skipped to the door with starlight in her eyes. "Come on, everyone's waiting."

Everyone? Who is everyone? And more importantly, who is he?

The questions formed in her mind like a slow-motion replay. She tried to speak, but words were impossible to say. She could only follow the girl to discover what she had implied.

The girl closed the door behind Harmony once her trailing gown cleared the threshold. There was no mistake in her mind about where she was—in the corridor of the Wentworth-by-the-Sea Hotel. The hotel's architecture reminded her of a wedding cake. As a girl, Harmony had dreamed of getting married here, but that dream died when they closed the hotel down in 1982. But how could that be? When had it been renovated? As these thoughts filled her head, she followed the girl down the hallway and paused at the top of the stairs.

"We're ready," the girl called down to a smartly dressed man speaking rapidly into a headset.

The man motioned for them to proceed.

Harmony took the steps slowly, trying to maneuver the multiple folds of the skirt without tripping down the stairs. Her eyes met those of the others who smiled up at her—a sneak peek at the bride.

The guests in the Wentworth lobby were dressed too casually to be attending a wedding. Since she was being ushered out the main portico, through the grand doors, she suspected the ceremony would take place on the lawn by the gazebo. The soft music from that direction confirmed her thoughts.

Immediately she tilted her head back, trying to catch a salty breeze or hear the cries of seagulls. Neither of those familiar sensations were present, striking further confusion in her mind. As her shoes touched the grass she looked back over her bare shoulder at the restored edifice of the hotel. Her eyes searching every detail; her brain wrapped around the image, trying to make sense of it. It glowed white, too white, and other additions were visible. What had they done to the Wentworth?

The instrumental melody changed. The girl at her elbow cooed breathlessly, "This is your special moment!" Harmony watched her move behind rows of elegantly dressed guests and walk up the aisle between the seats.

The man who'd been talking into his headset stepped up to her. "Your groom is waiting for you. You look lovely," he sang with joy. His hand on her back, he guided her to the location behind the chairs. The guests stood and turned to her. Again, the music changed.

As it filled her ears, her mind's eye pictured Kodiak—the man she loved. She couldn't wait to see him again, feel his arms around her. Eagerly she launched down the grassy path between the rows of strangers. She made an effort to find a familiar face, but she had never seen these people before. That didn't matter. What mattered was she was heading to see her groom. Perhaps they were renewing their vows in the human realm. Though she felt confused, everything would be fine once she was with Kodiak again.

The aisle seemed to never end as she trudged along, parallel to the length of the Wentworth hotel. Then she was relieved to see the gazebo just ahead. A man of the cloth stood in the shadow of the gazebo, as did her groom.

She was anxious, eager to see Kodiak, and quickly climbed the two steps. In her haste she stumbled, and her groom stepped forward, out of the shadows, to grasp her elbow. Grateful, she smiled up at him. But it wasn't Kodiak who caught her. A tremble rumbled through her before finally she was able to speak. "Suijin!"

Harmony's eyes snapped open. That wasn't the usual dream she had of Suijin. Too often, her dreams were terror-filled, and he wanted to drown her, not marry her.

She rolled her face into her pillow, grumbling that the mind was a fickle bitch! Today she was leaving Suijin to go back to her *husband,* Kodiak!

Harmony met Suijin at the water's edge, the city and palace at her back. She looped the satchel over her head and under her arm; it held a meager number of items she wanted to take with her. Leaving the palace after living there for so long felt strange.

During her last few strides across the gallery leading to the entrance, Luna had made herself known. Harmony wasn't going to stop or say anything to the siren who watched her egress. But the smug look on her youthful face forced Harmony to pause. "I know you're glad to see me go."

The siren's smile was deceivingly pretty, but Harmony knew better. Harmony couldn't stop herself from stating, "Take good care of him."

"Oh, I will." Luna's smile broadened.

Harmony had no right to feel jealous. After all, she was heading toward the arms of another man—that is, if he'd have her.

"Well," Harmony sighed, "I'll see you when I see you." And she left her nemesis and prison behind.

28

The Human Realm

Harmony maneuvered the waterways as effortlessly as the water god that swam beside her. Her expanding abilities, which had frightened her at first, were now comforting. She was adjusting to her place in this world—a goddess of sorts. However, she wasn't finished with her human life. It was time to write the final chapter with her husband, Kodiak; while he lived and breathed she wanted to be with him.

Though she had come to love the god alongside her, she knew he'd begrudgingly accepted her choice. How could he not? If he wanted to be with her in the long-term—sharing the extended life he'd granted her—then he had to let her go for a short while. *Short* being relative for a god who'd waited for someone to love since Earth's beginning. Harmony marveled at his patience.

After passing through the portal of broken water into the human realm, she followed Suijin down the eastern coast until they reached the tip of Florida. They surfaced in the tranquil waters off Key West. The sun hadn't yet lifted above the horizon, but the coming light promised its impending arrival. The sleeping town was still lit by streetlights, but no headlights roamed the roads. Suijin indicated they would swim ashore. While trepidation made her shaky, she followed him with long arm stokes until she was close enough for her toes to touch the soft sand. He stood and reached for her hand and towed her to the deserted beach.

Suijin stopped and silently turned, his torso facing hers. He gazed toward the horizon—the ocean, his home.

She studied his profile.

He is so beautifully constructed. But more than that, he is caring and thoughtful. His attentiveness toward me makes me feel revered and exceptionally loved.

"Jin" She sighed his name as she tugged on his hand, trying to bring his attention back to her at this critical moment. He was clearly lost in thought, but they needed to say their good-byes. His inhale confirmed he'd heard her, but he wouldn't look at her.

"Jin…" She conjured the words that she'd rehearsed in her head a hundred times. "No matter how far away I go I will never forget you. Whatever words I utter to another man or however long I stay away…" she paused, hoping he would look at her. He didn't. She continued with anguish and conviction. "I will always love you."

His eyes blinked slowly while his brow furrowed in distress.

"Jin, please look at me," she pleaded. She bit her bottom lip to stifle a groan. She had dreaded this moment, knowing it would be bittersweet. "I know you're not happy about this, but I have to go back to him. I love him too."

He turned to look at her then and growled, "I know!"

The flecks of gold in his midnight eyes looked like shooting stars. Her breath hitched. Oh, how she would miss looking into those ever-changing windows to his soul.

After an exasperated exhale, he let go of her hand. His fingertips brushed along her arm as they traveled upward to cup her face. His thumb brushed her bottom lip. Her mouth puckered to kiss the salty digit.

"When I'm ready I will come back to you," she promised.

"I will never be far from you," he vowed.

She shook her head and implored, "You agreed to let me go. Please, Jin—you must stay away. You can't interfere. *Can* you stay away?"

Harmony held her breath while he glanced again into the distance. The sun was cresting the horizon, and his irises adjusted to the brighter light by turning a pale ice-blue. Ice. She remembered when she'd first seen him after she fell through the ice as a child. The color seemed to mock her now. He was icing her out.

His gaze returned to her, but she wasn't looking at the color of his eyes any longer. No. Instead she watched his mouth as he stated, "I'll do what you ask. You won't see me again until you call for me."

She nodded. They were agreed. This was what she wanted.

His palm slipped from her cheek. He stepped back to leave her, but she rushed forward and grasped his arms. Hoarsely she cried, "Kiss me good-bye."

He was already pulling her into his arms, lifting her onto her tippy toes. Their mouths crushed together—two people expressing a love beyond words. Their lips lingered—brushing, recapturing, and caressing. His kisses spread to her chin and cheeks until she wound her arms even tighter around his neck. Hugging him fiercely, she buried her nose into his damp hair. She inhaled his unique scent, committing it to memory.

"Harmony...?"

The sound of her name presented as a question made her feel pathetic. He likely wanted to know why she wouldn't release him from her arms. She didn't want him to think she'd changed her mind. It was just...

Dammit, this is harder than I thought!

Her next words rushed out with finality. "Good-bye, Suijin. I love you."

She drew back and paused, awaiting his reaction.

He didn't say he loved her back. He'd said it before—plenty of times—but not now. All he said was, "Good-bye, Harmony Parker."

Iced out.

Suijin released her and turned toward the gentle waves. In a moment he was gone.

Iced out.

And she felt cold, and somehow vacant, both physically and emotionally. Harmony stood a long while staring into the sea, riding the waves of turmoil that raged inside her. Eventually she reminded herself she needed to focus on why she was here in Key West. Picturing Kodi's face, she felt calm, with a side of longing, overtake her. Finally, she would see him again after so long.

The sounds of motors, distant voices, and a barking dog seemed odd after the silence she'd experienced on Suijin's island. She had forgotten how noisy the human realm was. She adjusted her satchel and took a better look around. After a jogger gave her a strange look, she reached to touch her bare neck. From a distance the scales could pass as a tattoo, but not up close. Her sudden apprehension sent her back into the water to swim for a while. Suijin had told her that Kodiak had swum from this beach every morning for the past several months. She decided to wait and see if he'd come.

29

It was another sunny day in Key West. The hour was too early for summer tourists to be up and about on Duval Street. Harmony adjusted the gauzy white scarf over her hair and made sure it was wound securely around her neck. Her tunic covered her arms to her wrists, so all scales were covered. Her hair was mostly dry now. She'd stayed in the warm water watching her love take his morning swim. She hadn't been ready to reveal herself; her courage had faltered. Doubt secured her fear.

She concealed herself while Kodi sat on the beach watching the sunrise. She wished she could offer a penny for his thoughts. Did he wonder why she'd been gone a year? Did he want to see her again?

Harmony followed Kodiak down the narrow streets until he disappeared into a coffee shop. She waited for him to order and eat his breakfast. The longer she waited, the higher her anxiety reached.

What am I waiting for?

The dark sunglasses she wore, along with her scarf, probably made her stand out rather than remain a wallflower against the concrete building at her back. She hiked her unique waterproof bag farther up her shoulder and reached to remove her oversized, movie-star sunglasses. She pushed them up the bridge of her nose when someone opened the coffee shop door.

Kodiak waltzed out. Harmony's eyes followed his purposeful stride around the back of the shop into an alley. She rushed to cross the deserted lane and peeked around the wall into the alley. It dead-ended, revealing only dumpsters and an outdoor staircase that lead to a second-story apartment. Disappointed she'd lost him, she shuffled to the base of the steps.

Should I go up? Maybe he went up there?

"Harmony?"

At the sound of his voice she spun around, nearly jumping out her skin. Stepping from behind the dumpster was Kodiak holding an orange cat. The cat jumped from his arms when he stopped patting him mid-stroke. Neither human gave the feline a second glance.

"Is it you…?" He hesitantly stepped closer.

Harmony unconsciously slid the scarf from her golden hair and snagged the frame of her sunglasses. Drawing the glasses away slowly, she sent him a beseeching look.

He released a shaky and tormented breath as he rushed to her. "I can't believe it! I can't believe that you are here!"

"I found you! Are you happy to see me?" Her hesitant question was answered by his swooping kiss. When his hands plunged through her hair, she kissed him back. *He is glad to see me!* She was in heaven.

He broke the kiss to search her face. "Harmony, I saw your note and the herbs. I didn't think you were ever coming back. I waited—"

"I know! I know! So much has happened. I have so much to tell you." She glanced around the alley. "Is there somewhere we can talk?"

Coming out of his profound trance, he nodded toward the staircase and said, "My room is upstairs."

At her slight nod, he took her hand and led the way. The apartment was one room with a bed, dresser, and bistro table with two chairs. A darkened doorway on the far side of the room hinted at a bathroom. It was no more than a hotel would offer. "I've been here a few months. It's cheap, clean, and close to the beach. I've been diving and salvaging the wrecks off the coast for a local company," he explained, the brief version of why he was here in Key West renting this tiny dwelling. He indicated a seat at the table by the window, where the morning light provided meager cheeriness. Harmony sat down. He slid into the chair across from her.

The intensity of his copper eyes overwhelmed her. She was finally reunited with him, and there was no question of her love for him. It felt right to be here touching him. He hadn't let go of her hand, and their arms stretched across the lacquered table. His thumb brushed over the pearl ring that now symbolized their wedding, their union for this lifetime.

"So what made you go back? Did it have anything to do with Samantha's disappearance?" Kodiak's questions set her story in motion.

"Yes! Sam was abducted by a tribal Linker. He came for me but took her by mistake. Though I didn't know it until I found her in the other realm, I'd guessed there was foul play. After I crossed, Suijin took me to the island were Sam was held captive. And she wasn't alone—Finn was with her."

"The water god! Did he hurt you?"

"It wasn't like that!" She couldn't prevent the swift sting of tears. She shook her head, thinking that only a few hours ago she was kissing her other love good-bye. Blinking the tears back, she focused on the yellow building beyond the windowpane across the street.

"He helped me. It turns out he'd never wanted to hurt me." In a single moment memories flooded her mind. Repressing them, she returned her attention to Kodi. "But besides that—more importantly—the Linker who took Sam is Finn's father. Finn has both human and Aquapopulean blood, just like me."

"I guess that explains why you both have special abilities." Kodiak seemed to mull that over.

"His father thought if he brought me back to that realm, Finn and I would marry and continue a mixed-race family, securing the Linker's legend. Gale, Finn's father, came out of exile declaring Finn was his son, and he pushed to facilitate our union."

"You and *Finn*!" His shoulders hiked up as they tensed.

Kodi's jealousy toward Finn was evident. He obviously sensed the two shared something beyond friendship. Only it was kinship, not romance.

She eased his distress. "Gale's plan had a major flaw. He didn't count on Finn and Sam falling in love."

Kodi looked a little relieved, and he listened to her tale with interest. He seemed most surprised that Sam wanted to stay in the Aquapopulean realm, married to a tribal chieftain.

"What about Sam's dad? I told him you girls took a vacation, but then neither of you came back. I had your note, so at least I knew where you were, but I couldn't tell her dad that I thought his daughter was possibly in another realm."

"I know. I didn't mean to put you in that position. I witnessed their marriage in the tribal city and was on my way back to the Wellness-by-the-Sea to use the herbs and cross. Once home, I was supposed to tell Mr. Finch that Sam was unexpectedly called away to another job overseas. He'd believe it; you know how impulsive Sam is." Picturing Samantha Finch, her best friend in the world, she smiled slightly. "Apparently she's really happy, and they've had a child."

"Wow. So you were with them this past year?" She'd explained she'd been compelled to cross and help her friend, but why had she stayed so long? "Did you help her through her pregnancy? It would be the first mixed-race child born in the Aquapopulean realm. It must have been a joyous occasion."

She saw him struggle to understand. There was more to her now than her love for two men. It was time to reveal her physical changes. Would he accept the monster she'd become?

She gently squeezed his hand before she released it. With both hands, she clasped the scarf around her neck. "No, Kodi, I wasn't with Finn and Sam. I did not witness the birth of their child. I wasn't with clan family either. I was fulfilling an agreement I made with Suijin. He was the one who helped Finn, Sam, and I escape the Cape by providing us with a boat. In exchange, I agreed to spend time with him. You must understand our version of time versus an eternal god's is acutely different. I've been with him this past year."

"What would a god want with you, Harmony?" He failed to keep the accusation from his voice. He leaned back and crossed his arms.

"Kodi, you know I'm different. You've seen my abilities—I can deflect the sea serpents and Suijin with my magical force. You've seen me burn sirens. I've burned sea serpents and Suijin with my touch too. Please believe me when I say I wanted to come home to you every day. But there's more. I've been changing. Suijin is powerful and has given me the ability to hold my breath underwater like a clan Diver."

Like you—a renowned clan Diver. The same ability you lost when you followed me into this realm.

She read past his hooded expression; sadness and pain reflected in his eyes. He remained silent.

"I'm no longer afraid of deep water. I'm not afraid of drowning either because I can't drown. Suijin has also gifted me with eternal life." And then she slowly stood, unwinding the scarf from her neck. She held it in a fist at her side. Her other hand was splayed across her exposed neck, revealing the scales, revealing the truth.

He stood abruptly, upsetting his chair.

"Kodi, I don't know if we could make this work, but I'm yours if you will have me. If you can accept me...like this." She braced herself for his rejection,

216

knowing she was asking a lot. Admittedly she was an oddity, but she was still Harmony.

With one stride of his long legs, he reached her. He placed his hands on her waist in the old familiar way. "Harmony, I never stopped loving you despite our unconventional relationship. There is no doubt we can make it work. I'll do anything to make you happy. I'll quit diving if I need to so we can stay together. We can go back to New Hampshire. Anything. I love you."

Reassured and comforted that she'd made the right choices all along, Harmony released the scarf. As it fluttered to the floor, she skimmed her palms up his strong arms and secured them around his neck.

"I love you too."

They had once been strangers forced together by circumstance. She'd reluctantly made a business deal with him—his services in exchange for her precious heirloom ring. She'd vowed to dislike him. Their engagement was a sham invented to help them escape a murderer's clutches. Yet against all odds they fell in love.

Harmony met his kisses with the same longing and eagerness she received from him. Tears of joy spilled from her eyes and splashed off her chin. No matter what she had become, she would embrace it, nurture it. She wouldn't take any gifts she'd been given for granted— especially Kodiak's love.

Harmony would hold onto what she'd learned—if you don't sacrifice for what you want, what you want becomes the sacrifice.

EPILOGUE

2003
The Human Realm

Kodiak placed cash on the silver tray that was delivered with their brunch bill. He leaned back in the chair, resting his arm on the baluster railing beside their outdoor table. His wife looked lost in thought as she stared out over the back bay of New Castle.

Harmony Parker Night, you are so beautiful—more than the day I met you. Now thirty-seven, she hadn't changed much in the past fourteen years, except of course for the scales on her neck. Those seemed to have changed her on the inside as well. She wore a scarf whenever they were in public, as she did now. The gauzy fabric looked fashionable. The large-rimmed sunglasses perched on her head held her wavy blond hair back from her flawless face.

"I'm going to miss this place," she said. She stared off for a few more seconds before her gaze rested on him. "But I'm glad to be going home."

Kodiak smiled when she referred to the other realm as *home.* He was looking forward to going back and reuniting with his best friend, Rio, and the simple life among his race. Though Harmony had taken him through the portal many times, he hoped this would be the last.

After she had found him in Key West, they'd eventually returned to New Castle. She got a local part-time job and continued her efforts to save the historic building where they had enjoyed today's brunch. To their great relief, the Wentworth-by-the-Sea Hotel had been saved and restored, reopening its doors after twenty-one years.

A miracle.

"Are you ready?" He didn't want to rush her. This island and this hotel were huge parts of her past and meant so much to her. And they had recently sold her grandparents' house—her childhood home. They'd built their life together there over the years. Though he was often out working wrecks up and down the East Coast, her new abilities could take her to him, and his bed, whenever she wanted to swim to him. It was remarkable that his ability never returned and hers ultimately surpassed his. Not only could she hold her breath underwater for hours, but she could move through the ocean at a dizzying speed. She was truly transformed.

Suijin had taken her away from him, against her will, for more than a year and changed her into the goddess he wanted. Yet his wife had returned to him, professing her love. Kodiak couldn't sulk.

"Let's go home." She adjusted her scarf as she rose from her chair, slinging her purse strap onto her thin shoulder. Kodiak gathered his backpack as well.

They moved though the modern, tasteful lobby and out into the sunshine. He watched her look over her shoulder at the newly painted structure while they passed through the parking lot. They exchanged glances but kept moving. Their car, along with all their possessions, except the few items she kept in a safety deposit box, had been sold. They had spent this past week in a suite at the Wentworth Hotel. After checking out this morning they'd gone through the dining room to sit outside on the covered porch and eat their last human-cooked meal.

After a ten-minute walk through the woods they came to a deserted cove. Harmony set her bag on the ground and slipped into his arms.

"Kodi, I want you to consider moving to the tribal city after we go back."

"What? Why? I thought you liked the clan village. You could work in the library at the Wellness temple, like you mentioned. We can get a little house in the village. I can easily find work fishing." They had talked over these plans already. He realized Samantha and Finn were in the city, but moving there seemed extreme.

What he didn't know was that Harmony had sensed Suijin's presence, though he never showed himself. The god had stayed away, but he watched over her. Moving far from the coast would finally provide the separation she desired. One day she would return to Suijin, but for now she charted her path carefully.

Kodi grinned at her and said, "Ready when you are."

LEGENDS MATE (A WICCAN HAUS NOVEL)

Legends Mate is part of a multi-author stand-alone series. It tells the tale of a minor character, a scorned siren, from the Broken Water series who meets her—unlikely—mate.

Legends Mate

Scorned siren, Luna, seeks to heal her broken heart on the mystical Wiccan Haus Island, but she doesn't have a reservation. So, she sneaks onto the island, hoping they'll let her stay and rent a room. But there has been an assassination threat against one of the Wiccan Haus owners, and Luna's unscheduled arrival makes her a prime suspect.

Nate, a Sasquatch working for the Para-Elite Force, has come to the private island undercover, posing as a guest. He must flush out the assassin. When he's assigned to trail the hauntingly beautiful siren, everything goes sideways, and Nate is shaken to his core with yearning and desire. His soul mate could be the assassin, and he may have to choose between duty and love.

Author's Note

The idea that there could be something else out there...
in another realm or dimension, or in a world of spirits
has always fascinated me. And right here under my
feet—I think our planet's landscapes are miraculous. I'm
inspired by the creation around us. I'm also inspired by
how history and science shape humankind. In the
Broken Water series I used a scientific opinion on
evolution called the Aquatic Ape Theory for the
platform of building the Aquapopulean realm, which I
talk about in more in my author's note for *The Rare
Pearl*. I added a water god to go along with the water-
people I developed. When I was searching historic
beliefs and mythologies for a water god, I came across a
water god revered in Japan, Suijin. The meaning of
Suijin is water deity, but it also refers to a wide variety
of mythological and magical creatures found in lakes,
ponds, springs, and wells, including serpents (snakes and
dragons) and more. Suijin was an ideal god because my
Linkers were fascinated by the Asian Dynasties and
cultures and he fit well within the story parameters. In
the story, Suijin was cast to the earthly realms from the
universe, so his real name is unknown. To refer to him,
the Aquapopuleans named him Suijin.

In the human realm the story ends in 2003 at the
Wentworth-by-the-Sea hotel. I chose this year, because it
is the same year the Wentworth-by-the-Sea was *actually*
restored and reopened. At the hotel, I have enjoyed
many delicious meals in the dining and on the back
deck, which I wrote about in the epilogue. I humbly
hope my readers have enjoyed this imaginative series
that has crossed a variety of genres including science
fiction, fantasy, romance, mystery and adventure.

About the Author

Jennifer W. Smith is the author of the Landing in Love series. These contemporary small-town romances feature both sweet and sensual attractions. They always have something to do with aviation because this former flight attendant turned novelist has a flare for travel and adventure.

For adventure in a faraway land, check out her fantasy romances in the Broken Water series.

When not writing, Jennifer loves reading, talking to readers, and hanging out with her author friends. She lives in a quaint New England town with her husband and two children, along with their blue-eyed cat and rough collie.

Social Media Links

I'm always happy to hear from readers. Please let others know how you liked the book by leaving a review on Amazon.com and/or Goodreads.com (or other blogs and places you hangout on social media). A kind review goes a long way, and is greatly appreciated.

AMAZON AUTHOR PAGE Jennifer W. Smith

FACEBOOK authorjenniferwsmith

FACEBOOK GROUP Jennifer W. Smith's Book Squad

INSTAGRAM authorjenniferwsmith

GOODREADS Jennifer W. Smith

BOOKBUB AUTHOR PAGE Jennifer W. Smith

PINTEREST authorjensmith

Thanks for your support!